Dietrich Kalteis

The Get

A Crime Novel

Published by ECW Press
665 Gerrard Street East
Toronto, Ontario, Canada M4M 1Y2
416-694-3348 / info@ecwpress.com

Cover design: Made By Emblem
Author photo: Andrea Kalteis

LIBRARY AND ARCHIVES CANADA CATALOGUING IN PUBLICATION

Title: The get : a crime novel / Dietrich Kalteis.

Names: Kalteis, Dietrich, 1954- author.

Identifiers: Canadiana (print) 20230145728 | Canadiana (ebook) 20230145744

ISBN 978-1-77041-684-0 (softcover)
ISBN 978-1-77852-114-0 (ePub)
ISBN 978-1-77852-115-7 (PDF)
ISBN 978-1-77852-116-4 (Kindle)

Classification: LCC PS8621.A474 G48 2023 | DDC C813/.6—dc23

This book is funded in part by the Government of Canada. *Ce livre est financé en partie par le gouvernement du Canada.* We acknowledge the support of the Canada Council for the Arts. *Nous remercions le Conseil des arts du Canada de son soutien.* We acknowledge the funding support of the Ontario Arts Council (OAC), an agency of the Government of Ontario. We also acknowledge the support of the Government of Ontario through the Ontario Book Publishing Tax Credit, and through Ontario Creates.

PRINTED AND BOUND IN CANADA   PRINTING: MARQUIS   5   4   3   2   1

To Andie
always

. . . the mourning after

Two years of marriage and Lenny Ovitz was thinking of tying a different kind of knot — the one around his sweet angel's neck. Not something most guys think about back when they're saying their vows.

His Galaxie 500 sat parked the next street over, Lenny kept eyes across the tiny park, past the kids' swings and slide between him and their house, hoping to catch her coming out. Finger and thumb spinning his wedding band around the ring finger, replaying the rabbi's words: "Behold, you are consecrated to me with this ring . . ."

Talking to a sleazy lawyer about a divorce, Paulina was wanting to take Lenny to the cleaners, and he was guessing she had another man in the shadows. The reason he was parked there, hoping to catch her. Saying to himself, "Yeah, and I'm the bad guy."

It crossed his mind to save the time in court and the money on a lawyer. Be easier to just fix her: a car coming out of nowhere, or a mugging gone wrong. Or work up an alibi, then face her himself with his .32 and do it straight up. Yeah, he could do it, then sit shiva, put in the seven days. Move back into the house, lug the old recliner from the rafters, put it back in front of the Zenith, pull the side handle and up'd go his feet. Then hit the Bakelite buttons on the clicker.

No dividing the assets, and no hearing her kvetch how the chair's green vinyl didn't go with the room, or pointing her finger at the circles he left on the coffee table.

The porch light came on, something she did every time she left the house, and he lifted the Minolta by the strap, focused the telephoto and watched her through the lens, coming out alone and dressed casual with her racket, getting in her wagon, backing from the driveway and pulling away.

Setting the camera on the passenger seat, feeling irked for wasting his time, guessing by the outfit she was heading to the club to play her goddamn tennis. The ladies' club champ two years running — the woman with too much time on her hands — and Lenny paying the crazy membership fees so she could play with club pros who looked like Manuel Santana.

Starting his engine, he eased the Galaxie away. Thinking of her with some other guy, something that pissed him off. He'd been thinking if he could prove it, it would come in handy in the divorce proceedings. Now, he figured he'd skip all that, but he wanted to hear her deny it. Maybe he'd catch her, show her the snapshot, then plug her and maybe Manuel too.

Putting it from his mind, thinking he had time for a couple of collections before meeting his partner, Gabe Zoller, at the tenements near St. James Town, the new dumping ground for the poor. The slum block the two of them had bought, catching wind that the city was going to rezone for high-rises — Paulina not knowing anything about it — Lenny thinking of his own future, the extortion business not what it used to be.

. . . *shakedown street*

"**Y**ou oughta be shamefaced, what you do to your people." The tiny man looked at him, wiping his hands on the dirty apron stained with grime and poverty. But wiping wasn't doing much good. 1965: combat troops setting foot in Vietnam, Watts going up in flames, dead cosmonauts orbiting the Earth, and these people were living on sawdust floors, no heat and no hot water.

"Think you're my people, huh?" Gabe Zoller stepped out of the sun and into the doorway, letting his eyes and nose adjust to what lay inside — more a shack than a shop, not a wall that looked like he couldn't push a hand through it — swatting at the bottle flies buzzing around on account of the chickens and capons hanging in the front window. Its striped awning supposed to keep the light off the poultry. Live ones in crates clucking over by the chopping table, a tip of a cleaver sunk in the stained wooden top. One of the birds flapped, sending dust and feathers up into the thin stream of sunlight coming past the door. Gabe thinking the smell of the place belonged in a barn. More crates were lined and stacked out front. This guy whose name Gabe didn't remember, Kohn or Kahn or something, calling Gabe his people.

Collecting for Ernie Zimm, same way he did at the beginning of every month. This tiny man acting like he didn't know why Gabe was here, giving him the same hard-luck story about mouths to feed, showing the height of his kids with his hands, both children needing shoes. The guy's "oy oy oy" supposed to show the hardship. Three oys being a pretty bad week.

"We all got shit to schlep, man."

"God knows you and sees what you do." Kohn or Kahn pointed a knotted finger.

"God, huh?" Gabe let his eyes go around the place, saying, "You ask me, there's only you and me and the chickens." It pissed him off, this guy bringing God into it, telling him how it was. "Oughta take a hard look, and ask what God's done for you lately." Be doing a favor if He threw fire and brimstone down on this whole fucking ward. Burn it to the ground, as far as Gabe was concerned. A front room used as a store with a couple more rooms in back, one claptrap wall holding up the next. Gabe guessing the wife and kids were huddling back there, hearing through the thin walls, and staying out of sight.

Gabe gave another glance out the door. "You can run your mouth, but you still owe me the hundred." He snapped his fingers and put out his hand, eyes looking for anything of value. "Not gonna to ask again."

Two stooped old women in head scarves went by, both tapping canes on the sidewalk, careful not to look in, minding their own business.

"No more." Kohn or Kahn rose to full height and stomped a foot, top of his head up to Gabe's chin, his eyes defiant, shifting to the cleaver sticking in the carving table.

Gabe stepped to block him.

The tiny man jumped the other way and grabbed the push broom off the wall and stood with it like a rifle at present arms; this guy in his dirty apron was off his nut, giving Gabe attitude. Then he jabbed the end like a bayonet, and rushed at him, yelling.

Swatting the broom aside, Gabe caught the handle and tossed it away, then got a mittful of apron and spun the man, putting some weight behind the knuckles, slugging him in the ribs and sending him to the floor. Bending for the broom, he snapped the handle over his knee and tossed the pieces down, saying, "Okay, fun's over, I mean it. Let's have it." Wagging his fingers for the money.

"I ain't got it." The man stayed in a ball, holding his side.

When they copped an attitude, Gabe had to get tough, these old-world types going mulish about giving up their savings. Leaning down, Gabe slapped him across the mouth, saying, "You think it puts some pep in my day, having to smack you?" He grinned — yeah, it did. Catching the man by the apron straps, he propped him up. "How about now? Or you want more?"

The man's mouth was bleeding. Eyes slanting off sideways like he might pass out. Reaching in a pocket, he pulled some crumpled bills and held them out. "All I got, here take it. Take it."

And he did, Gabe counting it, then shaking him, making him dig in the other pocket, coming up with another deuce and some coins. Ended up just shy of forty bucks, Gabe made a face and shoved him back down.

The man gasped for air.

Wiping blood from his sleeve, Gabe pulled up the knees of his trousers and squatted back beside the man, saying, "I got a couple more stops to make, not the only mope I got to see. Was going for a drink after, now I got to stop off and put on a clean shirt, then come back here. Means I'm gonna miss happy hour."

The man's eyes lolled, Gabe not sure the guy was even hearing him.

"Pull it together, will you, man." Gabe could hear the crying coming from the back now. The guy's wife *shh*ing a child. "Look what you put your family through, selfish schmuck." Gabe lifted him by the apron straps and got him to his feet, clapped a hand on the boney shoulder, saying, "Okay, I'm gonna give you a break. I'm gonna be back end of the week. And I want the rest, you understand that? Every cent. Nod if you do. Okay then."

Shaking the shoulder, making the head bob back and forth.

"Letting you off easy, not charging interest this time, you understand?"

The man nodded, then made a sound in his throat like he might be sick.

Gabe let him go, the man tottering around, catching himself on the carving block, the cleaver stuck in the top.

It was a waste of time, trying to give a guy like this a break. Gabe watched the man as he considered the cleaver, then he collapsed back on the straw floor.

Saying to him, "Lenny, the guy I work with, wouldn't put up with this drek, not for a second. Can tell you that. He'd use his fists, then burn you out. You and everybody you got in back'd be out in the street. You understand that?"

The man groaned and gave a nod.

Hearing the wife and kids bawling in back, Gabe tossed the coins on the ground, the man snatching them up. Why did these old goats let their wooden heads get in the modern way of doing business. Seeing it as paying money under coercion instead of being kept safe from the riff-raff out there. A bad attitude, that's what it was.

Gabe checked his knuckles. Hands that used to be toughened from his time in the ring, now going soft. At one time he'd been in Ungerman's good books, the promotor finding him training at the Y on Brunswick Avenue, liked what he saw and put him in the ring, getting him a trainer, Gabe with a ten-and-six and lots of promise, sparred with Chuvalo, the two-time title challenger who was just another guy from the Junction. Man, that guy could hit from either side, left or right. They sparred head to head and toe to toe in '62, after George got himself disqualified for head-butting that Welsh fighter, Erskine. Say what you want about Chuvalo, that man could throw rockets out of nowhere that could knock you for a ten-count. Just ask Floyd Patterson about it. Gabe started making money on the side, doing collections for Ernie Zimm back then, not something Ungerman approved of, the two businessmen not seeing eye to eye.

Gabe hadn't stepped to the bag or into the club in months, nowhere near a hundred percent since he took the bullet earlier last year, caught it low in the abdomen, tearing up a mile of intestine. A shootout he and Lenny Ovitz got into with the Italians, guys trying to make Little Italy not so little. He left one of the Italianos, Marco DiPalma, breathing his last, and sent two of his crew running off, Lenny squatting behind the fender of Gabe's Catalina, firing across the hood. Gabe still wondering if the bullet he caught was one of Lenny's, the guy firing from behind him. Something he never mentioned. The two of them taking care of business, making their point — Ward Six belonged to Ernie Zimm.

Zimm had a med student make a back-door house call, a kid with some bad debts who didn't ask a lot of questions, patching Gabe up, told him he was the first guy he patched up since Yom Kippur. Ernie making Gabe pay the two hundred for getting the bullet dug out, along with the vial of painkillers.

Now, sucking his knuckles, Gabe was seeing the situation for what it was. He'd go back to the travel agency at day's end, the front for Ernie Zimm's operation, walk past Dag Malek and Manni Schiller sitting at their desks, and drop nine hundred and thirty-eight bucks in front of Ernie, having to explain why he came back light. Supposed to collect a hundred from each of the Market shops on his route. And he'd have to put up with Ernie going on about coming back light, calling it a miss. How he ought to take the rest out of Gabe's pay.

And when he found out Gabe laid a hand on this chicken guy, Ernie would give him more shit about his temper getting in the way of clear thinking again. Sure catching a lot of shit working for Ernie Zimm these days, and getting tired of the smug duo, Dag and Manni, desk jockeys always grinning when he walked in, like he was some joke. Dag with his stupid one-liners, the guy thinking he was Shecky Greene. The pair of them acting like the sun they promised their customers on those Miami cruises was shining from their assholes.

Guys with no clue what it was like down at street level, only a few blocks away from the Parliament house. Gabe wondering when was the last time Ernie himself came down to the Ward. Dag and Manni too, both gone soft in the belly, sitting behind those desks selling vacations, forgetting how to use their fists and strike the fear that once got them paid.

It was all him and Lenny Ovitz these days, the message was out around the Market, when Gabe "The Twist" or Lenny Ovitz came to collect, you paid what you owed. A miss meant getting thumped or worse. Gabe and Lenny in no mood to go back light, and Ernie Zimm not wanting to hear about it, writing the miss in his goddamn book.

Taking a trussed-up capon dangling in the front window, Gabe stepped out of there, into the squinting sunlight, crossing Nassau. A car with three guys inside squealed up short, and the driver tapped his horn, saying something out the window.

Thumping a fist on the hood, Gabe stepped to the driver's side, capon in his left hand, held it by the neck. "Know what happened to the last guy honked at me?" Looking at the two greasers in front, another in back. The one on the passenger side and the guy in back looking like brothers, same thick mustaches.

"That's good, except honking, that's a goose," the driver said, smiling. "What you got there's a chicken."

"What I got here's a capon." Holding it close to the guy's face.

The guy in back leaned forward, saying something to the driver, giving Gabe cold eyes.

The driver saying. "My mistake, a capon. A big bird, but no culhões."

"What's that?"

"You have yourself a nice day." The guy waving him off and driving on.

Going across to his Catalina, the Pontiac baking in the heat by the curb, a bullet hole still in the rocker, a reminder from the Italians.

Mid-June in Toronto, and it was like swimming in ball soup. He hadn't cracked the windows, thinking he'd only be a minute. Like an oven in the black car, Gabe laying the un-plucked bird on the opposite floor mat. Putting his back against the leather seat, sticking to it. Switching on the FM, pressing the middle button, the red needle jumping to 680. CHFI spinning some Percy Faith.

Not going to earn points with Ernie Zimm on the day. Ernie putting him on collections since he took the bullet. Ernie taking a lot of flack for the shootout, ex-mayor Phillips and local politicians making noise, demanding a crackdown on crime down in the Ward.

Collecting was getting to be a tough racket, the cops coming around and keeping an eye. The reason he went in on the tenement block by St. James Town with Lenny. The two of them borrowing heavy from Ungerman, giving up eight points. Lenny putting his own house up as collateral, doing it without his old lady knowing. Lenny and Gabe kicking out the low-renters and needle crowd, planning to get the apartments painted and cleaned up, then upping the rents, to go with the city's redevelopment of the adjoining blocks. Lenny calling it urban renewal. The revenue and increased property values promising to get them out of this life.

High time too. A month after the shootout with the Italians — Gabe still recovering — he limped into Hoffman's, the fishmonger on Baldwin. His sons catching him coming in the back, taking saps to him. Gabe punching his way out of there, firing a couple of blind shots through the stink of salt cod. Upping the crackdown into organized crime, putting Ernie Zimm's operation under the glass. Mayor Givens picking up the torch Phillips had thrown down, and not letting up. Ernie Zimm laying the blame on Gabe for that one. Gabe knowing his days with the outfit were in short supply. And now he was going back with a miss.

... *love means zero*

Paulina Ovitz smiled coming to the net, playing the good sport. Looking fine in her tennis whites.

This guy Gary Evans admitting she played a mean game. Tall and good-looking, he was saying, "It's about the workout, not the winning, am I right?" Smiling and making a clicking with his teeth.

"So they say." Paulina thinking the only thing she won was the spin of the racket, letting the match go best two of three sets, hoping none of the regulars had watched from the clubhouse.

Gary at the net, practically beaming, pretending like it didn't matter. Touching his racket to hers.

"Good match." Paulina smiled. This guy with the clicking teeth, all about the winning, guessing he didn't think it was showing. Taking the first game after the deuce, she made him pour it on, letting him think he had her chasing the ball from game to set to match. Paulina hitting them out, into the net, missing an easy ace. Playing the male ego, not the ball.

Now he was saying her game showed promise. Had played a half dozen times, calling her a natural. "Yeah, you had me going, that's for sure."

Watching him step to the bench, wiping the towel across his forehead. She said, "You hardly broke a sweat. Guess I'm not much of a challenge." Paulina being cute, thinking she could have beat him in straight sets, done it in her sleep, but guessed the eggshell ego was right behind the smile and clicking teeth. Something most men came equipped with, Paulina thinking she was an authority on it, married to Lenny Ovitz for two years that felt like twenty.

Making a show with the towel, Gary mopped his brow. His game more about flirting than competing — same way the game went each time he'd signed their names to the singles list. Playing the best two of three, once a week becoming twice a week. So far, he hadn't asked her out. She'd been letting Gary do the winning, but Paulina was wondering how he'd take a loss, thinking she wouldn't mind seeing how he handled it. Blitz him in straight sets, see if he was clicking his teeth then.

Wondering if he was married too, something about the guy that didn't sit right. In spite of the separation from Lenny, Paulina had left her own wedding band on. Maybe it was safety for when she wanted it, or maybe she was thinking it made her interesting, like forbidden fruit. Could be Gary left his own ring on the shelf in his locker. It wouldn't surprise her; the whole gender thinking from between its legs, those dangling little brains.

Smiling, she glanced to her bag on the bench, her towel next to it. Thinking she should take a wipe, at least act like she was glowing.

"What do you say to Friday, same time, give you a chance to catch up?" Gary smiled and clicked.

"But who's counting, right?"

"It's just a game."

"You know the club's got a couple of semi-pros, could give you a real game." She guessed what he was going to say.

"Yeah, but have they got heart?" His eyes shifted to her top, but he caught himself, looked back at her eyes.

Paulina thinking and touching her ring. "Really, that's the best you got?"

"So what say, I'll put us down, end of the week?"

"Long as you don't mind winning."

"One of these days, you're going to surprise me. I can feel it."

"Friday's good." God, she was sounding like a bimbo, like one of the club ladies she sometimes had drinks with, getting a kick out of their gabfests, mostly talking about what they owned, women they hated, or about the good-looking hunks at the club, or other stuff that made her yawn. Maybe she'd bring her game on Friday, go from love to game point and not let him up for air. Balls zipping past his racket. Paulina thinking, yeah, it might be fun.

He turned his wrist and checked the time, a Heuer Datemaster, not the top of the line, but not a bad watch, something she knew about. Learned from the best, her poppa running the finest jewelry and watch repair shop in town.

Gary surprising her with, "Hey, what say to brunch, on me?"

"Brunch?"

"All I know is Pauline, the girl with a lot of heart and a pretty good serve."

"It's Paulina, I'm hardly a girl, and that serve, well . . ." Nearly throwing in, "I could show you one you wouldn't believe."

"Good idea to work on that, the foundation of your game." Gary smiled, saying, "And sorry about the girl; you into it, the women's lib?"

"You mean like equal rights, the Pill, fair pay, all that?"

"Yeah, you know . . ."

"Not so you'd notice."

He nodded like that was good.

"You mind if I get wet while you get us a table?" Paulina still smiling.

"You bet." Clicking teeth.

Still smiling as he turned for the dining room. Paulina watched him go, remembering the Irish setter she grew up with. She'd throw a ball, and Rusty would chase it, bring it back to her.

Gary going to fetch them a table.

She called out to him, fifty feet between them, waiting till he turned back.

"You married, Gary?"

Looked like he'd been slapped, the way his neck went back.

"Me, no." Holding up his hand, no ring on the finger, saying, "How about you?"

"I don't know. Not really."

Clicking those teeth again, his smile wider and his head nodding like it was good. Turning back to get them a table.

Yeah, maybe Friday, she'd bring her game.

. . . *a little on the side*

Soon as he walked in the grocery, Lenny put Paulina out of his mind. Now dealing with this guy not wanting to pay.

"Come on, Serg, my man, you know how this works," Lenny flicked the long bangs from his eyes, wearing it modern the way men were doing these days. The boss, Ernie Zimm, said it wasn't right, a guy in his line of work looking like a Rosedale hairdresser. Lenny thinking it was just hair, plus what's the right look for a guy working extortion. So he had it a little long in front, still not the mop-top look of the Kinks.

Ernie was old school about it and not wanting his guys looking like punks doing the pick-ups, feeling there was a certain image management to the business of twisting arms. Lenny figured he got the job done, hair or no hair.

And here he was, feeling like he had to explain the game again to Sergio the shopkeeper, standing at the front of the produce market, thinking he was smelling cantaloupes, no customers in the store this time of the morning. Just the kid sweeping over by the tomatoes. Never had a problem making this stop in the past year, Sergio with the hundred ready under the leg of the cash register every time, handing it to him when Lenny showed up. Wishing him a good day, acting like he was getting value for his money.

Frowning now, Lenny said, "You're not going to cry poor mouth on me, are you, Serg?"

"It's not that," Sergio said, putting on a face like he was about to pass a stone. "We been doing business a while now, Lenny, and I like you fine. The thing is . . ."

"What's the thing?"

"There's these guys."

"What guys?" First thought was Gabe got his pick-ups mixed up again, stepping onto Lenny's route, doubling up on this guy. His partner not right since taking that bullet. Lenny feeling bad because he was pretty sure it was his bullet that put Gabe on the pavement, Lenny firing at the Italians, doing it from behind Gabe's Catalina, putting him in a crossfire.

"The Portagees," Sergio said.

"The what?"

"New outfit, they said. Told me to look around and count how many of your kind are still down here. Saying how most of you moved out long back."

"My kind?"

Sergio gave a look around, saying, "He meant Jews, no offense."

"That so, huh?"

Sergio sighed. "These guys walk in yesterday, early, and look around, you know, didn't buy anything, just told me I had to pay them now. One of 'em threw a cabbage." Pointing to where it struck the wall. "Other one hit me right here." A bruise showing under his cheekbone. "Asked where's my protection now. One doing the hitting asked what I was paying you, and I told him a hundred. Said he was okay with that."

"And you went along?"

"I got hit, right here." Sergio pointing again, then saying, "Look, I'm from Managua. Far as it goes, it's all the same who I pay. I like you, Lenny, always treated me good, all the time we been doing business. But these new guys say if I don't want things to go bad, like a fire, the kind of thing I don't want —"

"Where do I find these Portu-guys?"

Glancing past Lenny's shoulder to the front, Sergio looked like he just got a wedgie, straightening.

Lenny turned as three men were coming in, two splitting down the aisles looked like brothers, both with thick mustaches.

The one in the middle coming over, saying to Lenny, "You buying or selling, pal?"

"This the guy?" Lenny said to Sergio, looking the man over, thinking what a fucking time to leave his piece under the seat of the Galaxie, out at the curb. Saying to this greaser, a guy about his own size. "You think you know me?"

"Just some guy needs a haircut," the man said, his English pretty good. "A place up the street, got a red-and-white pole out front."

"Yeah, funny, that's my next stop."

"Not no more. You get it cut someplace else. You're done here."

"And who's telling me this?"

"I'm telling you, but could be you need a hearing aid too."

"Hearing's just fine, and I don't need glasses. I see just three guys. That it, the whole outfit?"

"Guess you got guys crouching by the lettuce, huh?"

"I can have five animals here in two minutes. Just takes a call."

"Yeah? Phone's over there. Think you'll make it?"

It was time to shut his mouth, but Lenny couldn't lose face in front of Sergio. He ought to get out of there and take the news back to Ernie Zimm. Let Ernie sort it out, likely send Lenny back with Gabe and they'd leave these greasers in the alley. And Lenny would be back next week, doing business as usual. But, then another thought floated in, and Lenny held it a moment, saying, "You know, maybe I see a way out of this."

"A way out?" The greaser grinned.

"Yeah, I mean for you."

The grin widened.

"Let's take it out back?" Lenny said, still putting on a show for Sergio.

"You and me, or all three?" The guy looked him up and down, likely checking for a piece under the jacket.

"You feel better, bring your mutts."

The guy looked to the other two and nodded, then said to Lenny, "It's your funeral." Cutting up the middle aisle, the other two circling around behind Lenny, letting him go ahead.

Lenny having second thoughts, but he was in it now. Hoping to get out the words before these guys started thinking of him as a pin cushion.

... *friendly fire*

G ary Evans looked at the change-room mirror, pushing the soap plunger to get it to work, rubbing soap on his hands, rinsing them under the faucet, pulling a paper towel. Thinking about Paulina Ovitz, smart, graceful on the court, a body that wouldn't quit. Sucking in his middle, studying the mirror, wondering if he was getting the onset of saddlebags. Pinching with his fingers. Thinking he better start working out or end up looking like Jackie Gleason. Too much surveillance duty did that to a man, sitting in his car long hours, peeing in a styro cup, eating Pop-Tarts cold out of the pack, and getting that one-armed tan, staking out the assholes.

Coming to the club the past several weeks, signing his name next to hers on the list, booking a court. Loved watching her play, the little grunt she made on a serve, the tone in her arms, the calves when she went up on her toes, the thighs showing below the white skirt, Gary burning for this woman, wedding band on her finger and all. He could barely keep score. And what kind of answer was that, not really. He'd ask her to explain it, maybe tell her how he'd been living with Abbie, both agreeing to call it quits after four years, now living like roommates, splitting the rent on the house, and sleeping in separate rooms.

Then reminding himself he was on the job, supposed to be mining information to take down Ernie Zimm's crew, nail them on racketeering and extortion. Gary there to dig dirt on her husband, Lenny Ovitz. Hoping to get him to turn and give up the rest of the operation for a reduced sentence.

Ernie Zimm being the top prize, the man like a plague on the Ward since he first stepped off the boat nearly twenty years ago.

Doing his job while toying with Paulina, Gary felt bad about the deceit, but couldn't help thinking about getting her in bed. Tossing the paper towel in the bin, he put on his shirt and walked out, buttoning it as he went down the carpeted hall, into the club's dining room and sat opposite, smiling as she read the menu, asking her, "So, what looks good?"

She nicked her head to the waiter serving a far table. "Benny says chicken à la king's the special. You tried it?"

"I stick to the Salisbury steak."

Benny came by, taking her menu, looking at him, asking, "The usual?" Calling him sir.

"Yeah, that sounds good, Benny."

"And put me down for the Caesar," she said. "And let's go with the tunnel of fudge after."

"Healthy and sinful," Benny beamed.

She smiled, looked to Gary, saying, "You behave, maybe I'll ask Benny to bring an extra fork."

Watching Benny leave, Gary was all smiles, saying to her, "You make it sound, I don't know . . ."

"Uh huh?"

"Dangerous."

"You're not afraid of something sweet, are you, Gary?"

"Dessert in the middle of the day?" He leaned back, still smiling, thinking of his love handles, saying, "I say bring it on."

"Here we are, two of us with no self-control." She was playing with him.

"Just don't see where you put it."

"The way you had me dogging the ball, I'm just gaining back lost calories." She grinned, then said, "Besides, we're splitting it."

' "No, no, it's on me."

"I meant dessert."

"Right."

"Divides the sin by half?"

He nodded, realized he forgot something, signaling to Benny again. Saying to her, "Wine?

"Already ordered it."

Gary smiled, about to ask what she meant when he asked if she was married. Paulina telling him, "I don't know. Not really."

. . . *a kind of soapbox*

Lenny Ovitz stepped out back of Sergio's, catching the rot of spoiling fruit in the bins, and maybe something worse, crates and bushels stacked against the brick wall. The only thing looking like a weapon was the lid of the trash can. He could punch his way out of a scrap, but there were three stepping out behind him, the two brothers fanning wide to flank him, knowing how this was done.

"You want to hear me out." Lenny held up a hand.

"You think it's got rules?" the one in the middle said.

"I'm looking for some guys."

"Guess you found 'em."

"Mean I might have a job."

"Yeah? You got ten seconds," the middle man said, holding up his own hand, slowing the brothers pulling razors, both making a show of flipping them open. Like they'd been watching *West Side Story*, leaving out the dance moves.

"Maybe you're the right guys, maybe not." Looking unfazed by the blades, Lenny said, "I need to put on a kind of show, like what you're doing now."

"Think maybe you're a little nuts."

"The three of you just walked in on Ernie Zimm's turf, and you think I'm nuts."

"How about we put your finger in a bag, one with the ring, send it to this Zimm, show him we're nuts, but serious."

"Then Ernie sends Gabe Zoller, the guy called The Twist, maybe you heard of him." Lenny hoping the name rang a bell. Adding, "Maybe a couple more guys. Then we see what ends up in a bag."

"This thing you're talking 'bout, putting on a show, why not use your own, this Twist guy maybe?"

"The man's all business, can't act to save his life."

"How much we talking?"

"Let's say a hundred bucks," Lenny said. "Just a show of muscle. An easy hundred."

"A hundred each, you mean."

Lenny frowned.

"We got a deal, or no?" The guy still holding up his hand, like he was set to let the dogs loose.

Glancing at the straight razors, Lenny said, "Yeah, guess I can go a hundred a man, but it better be a good show."

The guy in the middle looked at the brothers, then back to Lenny, relaxing his shoulders, saying, "We'll discuss it with our agent, but first . . ." And he caught Lenny flatfooted, rocketing a punch to his jaw, knocking him backwards over the trash can and down on his back. Lenny getting his feet under him, holding his jaw, thinking there was more coming.

The middle man turned for the door, saying, "Just so we understand each other." Then, opening the door, he added, "Get the cash and show up at the Lisbon Club. One hour. Oh, and you see that Twist guy, tell him he better watch out crossing the road."

And he went through the door, the others folding and pocketing the blades, following and closing the door behind them. Lenny hearing the lock turn from the inside.

Holding a hand to his eye, Lenny thinking the day was starting to shape up.

. . . *rent control*

"The fuck happened to you?" Gabe Zoller looked at Lenny, the two of them taking the rickety stairs, this place smelling rank. Gabe with the big ring of keys in his fist, one for every apartment on the block, a few skeleton rings on there for the utility rooms.

"Ah, you know, made this pick-up, and the guy failed to agree. Needed some tuning up."

Gabe nodded — nothing new there — left it at that and kept going up.

A stringy-haired drunk lay crosswise on the second-flight landing, bunched in a ratty coat, putting glassy eyes on them. Growling, he clutched his hands at a half-empty bottle, muttering at them.

Without a word, Lenny grabbed a handful of coat and called, "Cleared for takeoff," and flung the rummy past Gabe, man and bottle tumbling, the bottle bouncing around the landing below.

Looking at the spilled wine, the drunk snatched the bottle, which somehow hadn't shattered, got his feet under him and stumbled out of there, cursing them.

"How'd you talk me into this?" Gabe shook his head, couldn't believe he'd bought into these firetraps.

"Some fresh paint, we get her cleaned up." Lenny pointed to the ceiling, lath showing past missing chunks of plaster. "A bit of fixing, maybe brighter bulbs, and we're gonna turn this place around and double the rents. You'll see."

Gabe wasn't seeing it, going to the first door on the top floor, standing to the side, banging on it with his fist.

"The fuck you want?" From the far side of the door.

"Landlord."

"I ain't home."

"I'm counting to three." Gabe raised the big ring of keys, no idea which was the right one. Shrugging, he just stepped back.

"You oughta know what a man's holding in his hand before —"

Gabe kicked it in, his momentum taking him through the splintered door, banging into the man.

Stepping in behind him, past the broken jamb and twisted hinges, Lenny had the .32 in hand, looking around inside. The smell of garbage and piss.

"You said to three." The man reeled back, standing in filthy underpants, the waistband gone, one hand holding them up. The other pointing a finger at them.

Gabe swung and slugged him with the ring of keys.

The man folded over, underpants falling and tripping him as he stumbled back. Gabe grabbing him by his filthy hair, raising him to his toes and hitting him again with the keys. "That's two, you wanna go for three?"

"No, no." The guy threw up a hand, meaning no more. Limping to the kitchen sink, looking like he was going to throw up on the stack of dirty dishes. Instead, drawing a long-handled knife from the sink. Yelling, *"Ahhhhh!"* Charging, his arm going back in an arc.

Gabe caught him coming in, sidestepped the blade and slammed the keys against his skull.

The man went face-down, underwear around his ankles.

Gabe kicked the dirty knife spinning to the far wall, the blade sticking in the rotting baseboard.

Lenny stood over the man, saying, "It's moving day, 'less you got the rent, plus twenty for the door."

"I got shit." The man stayed down.

Gabe grabbed him by the hair again and got him up, tillering him naked for the smashed door, crashed him into the splintered jamb, saying, "Three."

The man stumbling out, splinters sticking from his belly.

"That's four, actually." Lenny kicked the filthy underpants after him, looked at a lumped bedroll on the floor, going over and swinging his foot against it, somebody moaning under it.

"That's my old lady." The naked guy called from the hallway, picking splinters from his elbow.

"She got the rent?"

"Maybe we can work something out." The woman looked up, smiling brown teeth at him.

"Get the fuck out." Lenny pointed to the door, the woman gathering her bedroll, hurrying past Gabe and his big ring of keys. Swinging them at her, smacking her on the ass, calling after them, "You come back, you're going out the window."

Lenny looked at the slop-covered two-burner, one of the elements gone, the hole with trash shoved in it. The sink clogged. Looked like there had been a grease fire going up one wall. Going to the window, opening it, he took a bag of trash and tossed it out. "I'm thinking we paint it yellow, something cheery. What do you think?"

"Yellow, huh?" Gabe looked at another pile of trash in the corner.

"This being the top floor, the penthouse," Lenny said. "Yeah, we clean her up, it'll fetch us a hundred and a half easy."

Gabe looked at the water-stained ceiling, more plaster missing, busted lath, wiring hanging from an exposed junction box.

"Yeah, a little fix-er-up, be good as new," Lenny said, still looking around, appraising.

Gabe was thinking of the cost of repairs, a dozen apartments in each of the three buildings, and the two hundred grand they borrowed from Ungerman. And how many years it would take to pay him off. Gabe looking at the door he'd kicked in.

"Property values around here are heading through the roof," Lenny said. "Just wait and see."

"Your wife know you bought it yet?" Gabe said, looking at the rotting ceiling.

"The princess? The woman thinks I'm the Antichrist lately. Hardly talks to me."

"You're a Jew, Lenny. You got no kind of Christ."

Lenny laughed.

"You didn't tell her, did you?" Gabe thinking maybe the princess gave Lenny the shiner.

. . . *the merchant of mink*

Borrowing a couple hundred grand from Ungerman, the man they called the Chicken King, going from poultry to boxing promotor. Buying up a few tenements of his own a few years back, used to take old "Boom Boom" from his boxing club and had him stand at the doors, the guy looking tough while Ungerman collected the rents.

Making the days' collections for Ernie Zimm, Gabe wondered how he'd let Lenny talk him into buying the three shit-holes. Borrowing and signing the papers Ungerman had drawn up. Real estate was a crime that was new to him. Gabe betting if Ernie Zimm got wind of it — his two collectors planning to get out of the life — no telling how he'd take it.

Last stop of the day had him looking for a parking spot along the side streets off Spadina, the garment district, the furrier calling himself the Merchant of Mink, half Greek, half Jew, with the Larry Fine hair, the man all of five feet tall, but a giant pain in the ass. And taking pleasure giving Gabe grief every time he came in, always starting with "So soon?" Doing the same routine, looking at his watch, loosening his tie, griping how Gabe was taking the shirt right off his back. The reason Gabe saved this guy for last.

The merchant not seeing Gabe as the last line of defense, keeping him safe from the eggplants and moolies set to jump from the bushes, hiding in the alleys. If not for Gabe and Lenny giving protection, the whole district would have gone to ghetto back when that kind started streaming in.

A nice place when Gabe was growing up, just known as the Ward back then. Everybody knowing everybody, kids playing street hockey, a lot of the families coming off the boats in the horse-and-wagon times. Building their houses and shops down here, their schools and places of worship. Gabe living with his folks in a flat over Peggy's Cigars, next to the Good Hotel, remembering how it stood crooked. Always figured it might tip into Peggy's some night. Gabe ready to hear a big crash, see bricks and glass raining through his bedroom window.

When the bureaucrats started leaving the back gate open, things slid down the crapper as far as Gabe could tell. A tapestry of culture and international flavor, they called it. People coming from the four corners, looking different, talking different, smelling different, letting houses go to ruin, their kids going to the same schools, mixing up the natural order. And now, what was left of his tribe — the ones who couldn't afford to move away — they didn't want to pay for protection.

He left Lenny on Queen, Gabe swinging his ass onto the Catalina's seat, looking at the sorry capon on the passenger floor as he pulled the door shut. Planned to give the bird to his landlady, have her pluck it and make soup. Lighting a Mark Ten, he steered around a pushcart hanging halfway into the street. A rack of men's dress shirts in crazy colors, some in polka dots, some striped, all with wide collars wagging in the wind, looking like they might take flight.

Switching on the radio, getting Roger Miller. Gabe tapped his fingers on the outside of the hot door, singing along about trailers for rent, and not having any cigarettes. Rolling west on Queen, he cut down a lane, going around a delivery van making a stop, pedestrians crossing like blind ants. Stop and go and hot as hell, getting to the garment district and looking for a parking spot. He ended up double-parking alongside a piece-of-shit Nash below Adelaide, putting on his four-ways.

Reaching in the glovebox, he took the Smith — he was never sure with these fur people, those little blades they had in their hands — tucking the piece behind his belt as he got out of the hot-box, stamping his fag on the pavement. Ignored somebody calling to him, grabbed his pack off the dash, looking up at the Victorian with the build-out in back. He went in the door, trudging up the stairs, holding the railing — no air and dim light in there — his shirt sticking to his back, with the sweat rings under the arms by the time he got to the third floor.

Going in the door, "Merchant of Mink" in gold leaf on the ribbed glass. Had to be ten degrees hotter up there.

The middle-aged woman sat at the desk, her black hair piled up, sweating like road crew and glancing from her ledger, looking over her cat glasses. Yeah, she knew who he was, and why he came.

"Tell him I'm here, huh, doll?" Gabe stuck another smoke in his mouth, flicking his lighter.

"He's busy." Talking in a nasal tone, she went back to her books, ignoring him.

"Come on, doll, I'm double-parked."

The woman pushed her bulk off her chair, those thick arms with the flapping skin, looking like they needed inflating. Stepped to a metal file cabinet, opened the top drawer, rifling through folders. Saying without looking up, "Told you not to call me that. And he can't see you."

"Can't or won't?" No way Gabe was going back to Zimm with two misses. One, okay, he could explain away the sixty-some odd bucks, but two misses . . . Walking into the travel agency, past Manni Schiller and Dag Malek next to him, the guy always cracking wise. Likely to come up with a line like, "Look, Ernie, no money, but Gabe brung you a chicken. Got his pick-ups mixed up with his take-outs."

The woman turned from the cabinet, used the folder to fan at his smoke, Gabe trying to move around her. The woman standing so she blocked him from the office door.

"Sure that's your move, doll?" Gabe said, smiling good-natured, flicking ash on the floor.

Stretching her arm without moving from the spot, she reached the phone receiver, saying, "How about I call the cops?"

He tore it from her hand and slammed it on the cradle, nudged her to the side, saying, "Woman, it's too hot to smack you one, but if you insist . . ."

"You goddamn crook." With both hands, she shoved him back a couple of steps, broke his cigarette.

"There you go." Tossing it down, he backhanded her across the mouth, her glasses flying, spinning along the floor to the water cooler, the wig knocked sideways, hanging half over the wild eyes trying to focus. Wiping spit and lipstick from the back of his hand.

And he was smiling, watching her sputter like she was drowning in a pool. Trying to straighten the wig, she was looking around the floor for her glasses.

"Allow me," Gabe picked them up, handed them back, then pushed past her to the office, the brass tag on the door: Cyd Doukas, *Private* under the name. He walked in, saying, "Cyd, my old pal, I'm here for what you —" And his hand was reaching behind his back, and he was diving for the wall.

Cyd Doukas was coming off the swivel chair, getting his pants pocket caught on the arm, throwing off his balance, trying to pull a nickel-plate from the drawer, almost had it aimed across the desk when Gabe shot him in the chest, planting Cyd back in the swivel chair, nearly tipping him backwards, the body bobbing back, then forth. A big red pock on the white shirt. The balding head flopping onto the desk. The man never said a word, just tried to shoot him.

Gabe stepped in, pointing the barrel at the back of the man's crown. But it was done. Red all over the desk blotter. Had to be the fucking heat in this place, making these people crazy.

Meaning Gabe was going back with two misses. And nearly got shot for the second time in a year — if the guy's pocket hadn't got caught on the drawer and thrown him off balance. He turned, the big woman frozen at the door, couldn't believe what she was seeing, then backing for the water cooler, her brain searching for that scream, her fat arms clutching the folder in front like a shield.

"Anybody out back?" Gabe asked.

Her mouth dropped open like she was about to wail opera, and Gabe put one through the manilla cover, knocking her into the water cooler, the glass jug smashing to the floor. The big woman spun once and took a graceless bounce off the wall and down she went, the wig tumbling off, the wig cap making her look balder than Cyd, her blood mixing with the water on the floor.

Going to the workroom door, he had a glance inside. Bent and looked for feet showing under the work tables. Nobody in there. Checking the drawers of both desks, then the filing cabinet for payroll cash, coming up empty, he hot-footed it down the three flights, getting out of there before anybody came asking questions. No time to grab a fox or mink off a rack in back for the landlady. Two misses and a chicken, the meat likely spoiling on the floor of his Catalina. Hadn't cracked the car windows, not in this neighborhood.

. . . omertà

Wasn't proud of himself for stringing her along. Paulina was still married, yet going to brunch with him after tennis, asking if he was married. He found out she was done with Lenny Ovitz, not going home to a crook like that, a two-bit bloodsucker working for Ernie Zimm, doing collections, running a late-night poker game over in the Junction. Believed to be involved in the shooting death of Marco DiPalma, with another piece of work who worked for Zimm, Gabe Zoller, a guy they called The Twist. Gary keeping both of them under surveillance.

Gary having a good time getting to know her, the two of them digging spoons into the chocolate. What started out as a job had become a game, Gary getting the idea it was leading to her bed, one lying step at a time. Poking around for information and gaining her trust. Tried telling himself he was doing her a favor, putting a guy like Lenny behind bars. Gary working undercover while getting under the covers. The badge not making him feel like the good guy in this. And when she found out he didn't teach science at Jarvis like he told her, it would be over, and he'd just be another bum lying to get what he wanted from her.

Now Gary was walking through the doors of 52 Division, burping chocolate, on his way to see the lieut to give his update. Not much to tell at this point, just that he'd been gaining trust with the wife of Ovitz. Gary telling the lieut he doubted she knew much about her husband's activities, just that the guy had been going out the door every morning to work at the travel agency, the surveillance team keeping an eye from across the street, upstairs of the Caribbean place. The lieut asked if the woman was blonde, meaning dumb. Gary telling him yes and no, blonde but not dumb. The lieut telling him to stay on it and keep digging.

"You bet, Lieutenant." Going and sitting at his desk in the shared office down the hall, Gary added to the file. Names on his pad of guys working for Ernie Zimm: Dag Malek, Manni Schiller, Gabe "The Twist" Zoller topping the list. All Lenny Ovitz had on his sheet was a teen arrest for car theft that didn't stick, Lenny jacking a VW Transporter the night of his bar mitzvah, back before he was even shaving. Packing the van with his pals, the joyride fueled by Manischewitz and Benzedrine ended with the van hugging a lamppost, bleeding fluids. Lenny ended with a mild concussion, the girl called Esther, sitting next to him in the front, ended with a chipped tooth and a couple of bruised ribs. Booked for driving without a license, drunk and disorderly, along with public mischief, Lenny trying to rip the VW logo off the crumpled front, telling the officers arriving on the scene he did it on account the damned thing was designed by Hitler, and he was sick of that fucking guy. The judge leaned across the bench telling young Lenny he ought to pay more attention in class, that madman had been doused and gone up in flames years ago, banging the gavel, sending Lenny for psychiatric evaluation. Charges against him were dropped on account he was thirteen at the time. Nearly twenty-five years ago now. And nothing since.

Gary lifted Lenny's photo from the file, one the surveillance guys snapped as Lenny crossed the street from Zimm's, going into the Caribbean place for coffee. Gary thinking, you don't walk this time. Lenny Ovitz had a comet of justice coming. Then wondered some more how a smart woman like Paulina ended up settling for a guy like that.

. . . *the mantrap*

"Since when do I need a gun?" Isaac Levine held his hands wide and smiled at Paulina, his daughter, the apple of his eye. Setting down the paper bag she'd picked up from Mica's deli, taking a detour after tennis at the club, supporting her cousin's new venture.

"You're changing the subject, aren't you, Poppa?" She acted like it was cute what he was doing, the daughter playing along. She loved working at the store, their banter and their times together, learning the trade from him. Her poppa the best jeweler in the city — wasn't anything he didn't know about fine watches — could strip down a Rolex, work the tiny tweezers and screwdrivers and put it back together better than new — and what didn't he know about diamonds and gold?

"I'm talking about a little security, and you want me shooting guns." He smiled back, his little ketsele with the two-shot pistol in her handbag. He turned to the portable Zenith that usually kept him company, the dial set on CKEY. Sinatra filling the store, the crooner letting the world know he was starting to see the light. Isaac turned it down.

44

"I didn't say you had to shoot somebody," she said. "What I asked about were these doors." Not letting him off the hook. She looked at the mantrap doors he'd had installed last week, the controlled entry system into the store, a dead space between doors of bulletproof glass, one closing before the second one could be opened. Maybe something he saw on *The Man From U.N.C.L.E.* The camera, called a closed circuit, completed the paranoia. The locks controlled from behind Isaac's counter. Saying to him, "One thing's sure, a gun's cheaper." Looking at the forbidding doors with the bulletproof glass. An ugly way to enter into a place that sold beauty.

Isaac's Jewelers since 1946 lettered across the glass front. Not the year Isaac opened the business, but the year he stepped off the boat and into his new life in a free land. Not as one of the liberating heroes returning home, but one of the liberated. Isaac Levine who one time had dreams of being an Olympic gymnast, with his practical side set on becoming a fine watchmaker, learning under the eye of Laslo Pfeffer, a master craftsman, learning in the man's storefront shop in the heart of Budapest. Training for hours at the gymnasium before daylight, straight-arm work on the still rings, the weighted chins, followed by a twelve-hour workday, learning the trade. Isaac never tiring, loving every minute.

After the dark shadow of hell fell across Europe, his family, along with the Pfeffers, were thrown onto the cobble-stones out front by the Hungarian police. Never to see his mother and father and older sister again, he was locked up and beaten and eventually forced onto a train's cattle car with no food or water. Long days of being an apprentice became longer ones of forced labor, more beatings and untold cruelty. The six digits roughly tattooed on his arm. His physical stamina dissolved, yet somewhere inside a young Isaac found the resolve to survive. Nearly a year in that camp in Hungary before he was moved to one on the outskirts of Austria. Arriving by locomotive in the middle of the night, a place with an iron gate outside that read: *Arbeit macht frei.* Isaac was told by another prisoner, "Look, no chimney." The man smiling, explaining if they died it would be from labor, not gas.

Half his body weight gone, Isaac's resolve was tested every hour of every day, and he endured whatever the guards and capos did to him, and he pushed from his mind what they forced him to see. They beat him more when he refused to become a capo — not taking part in creating more misery for his own kind — and somehow he stayed on his bare feet, and ended up among those left standing in the filthy rags, barely seventy pounds of man clutching the perimeter fence, the camp finally abandoned to the Allied troops.

Spared by the typhus that had taken so many, he was treated in a medical tent. A British nurse dubbing him the tough goat, the young man impossibly sick and weak, but never letting go of life. Always smiled at the hospital staff.

One fevered night, he got off his cot and moved between the rows, found one of the capos who had tormented them, rewarding him with a trip to the promised land, for what he did to his own people. Isaac doing it with his bare hands.

The nurse on morning rounds found the capo tipped from his cot and onto the floor, his eyes bulging and his tongue hanging out. The man on the closest cot swore that the man got up and cried in the night, said he couldn't live with himself for what he did, and he strangled himself. Nobody asking any more questions.

When Isaac was well enough to travel, he was moved again. The British staff putting him on another train. This time headed for a DP camp at a place called Mannheim, where they gave him three meals a day and more of the medical attention he needed, and by the time he doubled his weight, his papers arrived from one of the countries that had refused Laslo Pfeffer and his own family entry just a decade earlier.

With his newfound refugee status, Isaac left the rubble and madness of a country being quartered, and he stepped on a transatlantic steamer, the *Arosa Sun*, and landed at the port of Quebec. A man alone in a strange new place, never to hear about his own family or from Laslo Pfeffer ever again.

Speaking no French, but with enough English to declare he wasn't a communist, Isaac had his papers stamped and was relocated to downtown Toronto and housed in a flat with four other men, two of them Poles, a Hungarian and a Czech. And he was sent to stand in an employment line every morning, hoping for work and taking whatever he could get, laying bricks, road crew, unloading ships on the Quay. It didn't matter. Isaac Levine was earning his way in this new world. And all that darkness was left behind, and he vowed to never speak of it again.

The first autumn in the new world, as the leaves turned golden, he met his Helen at a shidduch, and he knew by looking at her they'd have a life together. And many years later, she admitted she knew it too. They were married in a small ceremony as the leaves returned the following spring, and they were never apart after that. And they worked hard, Helen as a caterer, and Isaac working construction jobs and repairing watches after a ten-hour shift on whatever job site he'd been sent to. Replacing crystals and movements with his rough hands and getting broken watches telling time again. Selling refurbished ones from a shared market stall on weekends until they could afford the one-bedroom off Spadina, where he opened his own door, doing an honest trade, building a reputation from his parlor room. And a year later, they were blessed with the best news of all, Helen's eyes alive and dancing as she told him he was going to be a poppa.

And he worked even harder so Helen could eventually stay home with the baby, and the locals came to know him as Isaac the Jeweler, a man who knew his trade, and one you could trust. Isaac making the ends meet, and finally moving Helen and Paulina, still a toddler then, to the house on Spadina, the business in the front room, their living quarters upstairs. Paulina in the fifth grade by the time they sold that place and afforded the house Helen had fallen in love with in Forest Hill, seeing a picture of it in a realtor's window and stirring up the courage to enter and enquire about it, telling Isaac about it that night over supper.

And he came home ahead of her birthday and told her he had a problem, couldn't find a ribbon long enough for her gift, smiling as he handed her the keys to the house. Looking in her eyes as she figured out what he meant, seeing his Helen crying with joy.

Renting a store on nearby Lawrence allowed him to come home for lunch with his girls. Better shops, better schools, and a safer neighborhood. He went on fixing watches, and selling the latest by Jaeger-LeCoultre and Rolex and Breitling from his shop. And he added jewelry from the House of Chopard, Bulgari and Tiffany. And their life together blossomed and it was all good.

"We have insurance, Poppa," Paulina said, still on about the mantrap, looking at the doors.

"And now lower premiums," he said. "Pays for itself in five years, six tops. You're going to see." He waved a hand in the air like it was already done.

She pointed to the front, saying, "And what kind of name is that, 'mantrap'?"

"A good name. Exactly what it does, it traps."

"Traps your customers?" She laughed, taking the wrapped sandwiches from the bag. "Don't stand there, buy something. Then you can leave."

Isaac loved her sense of humor. Told himself it's what kept him going. Pinching a dill spear, he took a bite, then tried changing the subject. "This from Mica's?"

"Where else?"

"Got to admit, the boy works hard, he'll give the rest a run for their money. Mark it down." Isaac looked at the sandwiches she took from the bag, piled high with meat, a half inch extra for family.

"Everyone knows you, Poppa. Isaac the Jeweler." Paulina not swayed from the conversation, saying, "Who would even think of robbing you?"

He smiled at her: beautiful and smart, but maybe a touch naïve. Saying, "And you with a gun in your purse."

"It's a derringer, Poppa. A lot of jewelers carry these days. It's almost stylish."

"But you do the books, Schatz."

"Think the crooks know it?"

"And you can shoot?"

"Yes, I can shoot, and stop changing the subject, and tell me, how much?"

And his smile widened. Yes, just like his Helen. God, he missed her, but it felt like she was living in this girl, a mirror image of his darling wife.

"You look at me like that, Poppa — like I'm your little girl — I already know it's too expensive." She folded her arms, trying to look stern. Paulina steadfast as a hound, going to find out what the mantrap cost.

"Eat your lunch, ketsele," he said, smiling. "Not like I can send the doors back."

49

"I'll have to enter it in the books."

"Yes, you'll find out in time, but now, let's eat." He finished the spear of pickle, tapping the glass display of bracelets and necklaces. "Let me show you the Buccellati, just came in. And here, the Cartier Panther, white gold and emerald eyes. What do you think?"

"I think I'm going to eat." She didn't look at the case, her eyes going from her sandwich back to those doors. Saying, "I mean, if we can still afford food." Adding, "But you know I will find out."

"Of course you will, Schatz."

When she'd come in with the take-out, Isaac had trapped her between the doors, daughter calling the father a child, the two of them playing. Now they sat on either side of the Rolex case. Isaac saying, "So no more talk of mantraps or Italian gold. Aside from a good lunch, what else is there?" He was trying to rekindle an earlier conversation.

"I love having lunch with you, Poppa. You know that." She set the wrapped sandwiches on top, along with the remaining dill spears. Setting his sandwich in front of him, the pastrami piled high between the marble rye.

Paulina saying Mica's wasn't busy ahead of the noon rush, and it kind of worried her.

"Like I said, he'll do fine. Now, you were saying something about you and Lenny . . ." Looking at her.

She frowned, almost wished she hadn't hinted her marriage was past sinking when he asked how things were when she first came in, Paulina turning the talk to the mantrap doors. Now looking at the sandwiches, pastrami for him, sliced turkey for her, reaching the wax-paper-wrapped rugelach from the bag, taking her time, saying, "He's out."

"Of the house?" Isaac looking surprised, hiding the pleasure in hearing it.

"You knew it all along, didn't you?"

He waved a hand, saying, "Never saw the kismet, no, but you have to listen to your heart, ketsele, not to an old man."

"Or to my dumb head either."

"Okay, you said it." He reached for the cloth under the glass, set it on top and smoothed the corners, eyeing the rugelach.

Paulina saying, "I wish there was more we could do for him than buy a sandwich."

"I tried to tell him, with the Zuchter's and Wexler's and Pancer's. Over a dozen more. And all of them here since the Depression. Could've gone into something else, maybe appliances like Mel with his Bad Boy place. But hey, Mica's young and stubborn," Isaac said, waving his hand. "Like I said, he'll do fine."

"Reminds me of you."

"I was determined." He admitted it, picked up the sandwich in both hands, winking at her and taking a bite.

"Just wish there was something . . ." She waved a hand, guessing he was right, Mica would make his own way. Knowing how her poppa settled here at a time when there were still rumors of swastika clubs and signs in shops telling him his kind and dogs weren't welcome.

But he never talked about any of that, just the stories about when he met her mother at a social, how he knew she was for him, first time he saw her. Walking his Helen home when they were just dating, hoping for a kiss at her door. How he didn't have much to offer back then, but who did? Said he never understood what the woman saw in him in the first place, but there was something, that spark between them. How his Helen believed in him, and wanted to have his children. And not long after the baby came, he had saved enough to move them to Forest Hill, the house she'd seen advertised in that realtor's window. And they'd been happy and prospered. Yeah, Paulina knew all those stories, could almost tell them word for word herself. And she had plenty of good memories growing up: the schools, the camping holidays in the Kawarthas, those picnics by Lake Simcoe, driving up in the old blue-and-white Chevy. The summer drives to Florida, that little motel by the ocean.

She knew he missed his Helen as much as she did, two years since her mother had been gone. Her clothes still hanging in her closet, like he was waiting for her to come back. All those framed photos over the mantel.

Eddy Arnold coming on the portable radio now, making the world go away. Wanting to spare herself from the melancholy of thinking about those yesterdays, she steered their talk, saying, "Well, you ask me, a nephew needs his uncle."

"My door's open. He knows that."

She looked at the mantrap doors. "Yes, a real welcome."

Isaac smiled. "Mica could have gone to college, been a tailor and joined the needle trades." Isaac talking about the Tailor Project, the country still looking for laborers, first plucking them from the DP camps in Europe. "Never too late."

"He wants life on his own terms, just like you did, Poppa."

"Then what does he need me for?" Isaac taking another bite, saying the boy did make a fine sandwich.

"You're such a billygoat." She shook her head at him, told him to stop eyeing the rugelach and eat his pastrami, offering him the last spear of pickle.

... *backfire*

Gabe Zoller opened his car door, got in and sat on the baking leather — like a fucking schvitz — cranked down the Catalina's window and turned the key, dropped it in gear and pulled away from the two-tone Nash he'd blocked in, two spinsters inside gawking at him, one giving him the finger. Drove to the first intersection when he heard the siren, blocks away but getting closer.

Gunshots from inside the Merchant of Mink getting the blue boys' attention. Could be Gabe missed an employee hiding in back, or that sweaty woman tripped an alarm under the desk when he ended Cyd Doukas. Hanging his arm out the window, telling himself to take it easy, just a guy cruising. The cops were likely responding to a "shots fired" call, couldn't know more than that. Rolling up the block when the first yellow cop car showed at the intersection ahead and pulled across and blocked the lanes, its gum ball spinning red on top. The cop inside looking this way.

Putting on his signal, Gabe turned right into the mouth of an alley, a delivery truck with its tailgate down blocked the exit. Looking in his rearview, he caught more flashing lights, another squad car coming from behind him, boxing him in. Reaching his .38, he shoved it into the cavity of the capon. Getting out, holding the bird like an extension of his wrist. Looking for someplace to toss it.

Pulling the handle on the only door down the bricked alley — locked — he turned, seeing the cops getting out of their squad cars and coming at a trot, both of them unholstering duty weapons. The first one had a two-handed grip, taking a bead on Gabe, shouting, "Get your hands in the air, get down on the ground — and don't fucking move."

"One at a time or all at once?" Gabe held his hands wide, the poultry at arm's length.

"Hands where I can see them," the cop barked, an unsure look at the bird.

Turning to face him, Gabe caught the other cop in his periphery, coming past his Catalina. Gabe saying, "I see the problem, officer. I'm blocking the alley. Was only gonna be a minute."

The second cop rushed from behind, same two-handed grip on his weapon, yelling, "Drop it."

Gabe looked at the capon like he forgot it was there, his hand around the pistol grip halfway inside the bird, finger on the trigger. "Was gonna drop it in a pot."

"Last time I tell you. Drop it!" The first cop closed the distance, aiming at Gabe's chest.

His hand in the cavity, Gabe turned slowly to the one behind him. "You want me dropping my supper on the ground?"

"Do it, now!" The first cop holstered his piece, took his nightstick and swung at his wrist, knocking the capon away. Then grabbing Gabe's arm, both cops shoving him into the bricks, his arm cranked high behind his back.

"What the fuck . . ." Gabe knowing better than to struggle.

One cop telling him, "Shut your trap and hear your bill of fucking rights." Twisting the arm higher, had Gabe on his toes, reciting the words, ratcheting the cuffs good and tight. The other one patted him down, then forcing him to his knees, using a boot to push him down, face to the wall.

Unable to break his fall, Gabe felt his head hit the bricks, then the asphalt, a hot-piss funk filling his nostrils. The cops standing over him, taking their time now, Gabe looking at the spoiled capon lying in a puddle, its feathers looking mangled. Saying, "This ain't kosher."

"Shut the fuck up." One of them kicked the bird, and the pistol clattered out onto the sidewalk.

The other cop saying, "Well, well . . ."

"I thought it was the giblets." Feeling himself jerked to a sitting position, a hand grabbing his collar. Gabe saying, "You boys mind calling my landlady, tell her to order in Chinese." Saw the cop's fist coming, nothing he could do about it but turn his cheek.

. . . katz meow

Walking into Mica's deli, the bell jingling over Lenny's head. Shelves down both sides and a glass counter at the end. The place in need of some decorating, the aroma of something pickled. Paulina's cousin with the white cap on his head, supposed to make him look like the cook. Lenny feeling good about his plan, saying, "Hey, Mica, how's it going?"

"Hey yourself, Lenny. You're the second Ovitz in the last hour." Mica Katz looking glad to see him.

"That so?"

"Missed Paulina by this much." Mica's eyes went from smiling, taking on their usual serious gaze, magnified by the thick lenses. Sighing like he was deflating, then saying, "It's been lousy, if you want the truth."

"Sorry to hear it." Lenny knowing the guy would go on, couldn't help himself.

"You too, huh, by the look of your eye?"

"Banged the medicine cabinet. Nothing really. So, Paulina was in, uh, getting lunch for the old boy?"

"Sliced turkey for her, pastrami for him."

"Folks got to eat, right?"

Mica puffed a sigh, saying, "And by lousy, I mean dead the whole week."

"You can't help it, can you?" Lenny couldn't believe this guy was related to Paulina, a first cousin on the maternal side. Chubby with nothing that would pass for muscle, not even man-hair on his arms, looked like two eyes and a mouth stuffed into sausage casing. Lenny wondered if he shaved. The pop-bottle glasses giving him the blink of an owl — the poster boy for pity.

"I'm just talking honest," Mica said.

"Think you're the only one with problems?"

"You don't want to know." Mica shook his head, muttering, "Oy oy."

"Bit of advice for you, a regular comes in, sugar it up a bit, huh? They ask how you're doing, don't depress the hell out of them."

"You're family, Lenny, we got no secrets."

"Lucky me." Lenny looked around, past the window to the street, asking where Mica kept the horseradish. He didn't share much with the family, liked to keep his business to himself, especially the way these people dished the dirt. Who knows what the little wife let out of the bag.

"So, that eye, come on — Paulina pop you one?" Mica winked, then pointed to a shelf on Lenny's left.

"My sweet angel, you kidding?" Stepping to the shelves. "The girl's all hugs and kisses when I come home."

Mica shook his head, saying, "Tell you, a week like I had, I'm feeling like I can't sell brisket to a Jew."

"See, right there. I come in for deli, tell you to can it, you give me a side of grief."

"Okay, forget it."

"Ever hear of rose glasses? Ought to get a pair, put them on once in a while, look at the bright side."

"Yeah, guess you're right, Lenny." Mica smiled again, saying, "Come on, who popped you?"

"Told you, I bumped the wall."

"Mean the medicine cabinet."

"Bit of this, bit of that, banged it, bumped it, who gives a shit." Repeated he just stopped in for something to eat, helping Mica out. Had to be a dozen other places Lenny could have gone for deli, all within a few blocks. But none that would work into his plan. Glancing at his watch, he said, "Look at your Uncle Isaac, how he started out."

"Oh, God, I hear one more Isaac story ..." Mica rolled his eyes. "The man surviving typhoid —"

"Typhus."

"How he came over with just the clothes on his back."

"Yeah, I know that one." Lenny shook his head. He'd heard them all too, everybody in the family telling tales of Isaac; everybody except Isaac. The man never talked about what he went through. The one time Lenny asked about surviving the camps, Isaac told him, "The past is the past, and tomorrow, who knows, but right now is where I live. End of story."

Looking out the front window, guessing he had another minute, Lenny shared a tale about his grandfather Lesham coming from Hungary around the turn of the century, opening a milk store from a cart out front of his shack. Not allowed to sell to the Brits or Irish back then, Lesham sold to the new immigrants flooding into the area, anybody wanting milk and cheese. Outgrowing the cart, Lesham got an old van, hired a couple of local boys to make deliveries. Finally opened a store and branched into imported specialties. Going strong by the time of the sausage houses and kasha and hotpot joints and roti carts that came much later, the dhansak and jalfrezi after that.

The whole world opening its culinary doors down in the

Ward, selling their goods off the back of crates and boxes out front of their shop windows, bushels and aromas along the sidewalks of the streets lined with cars down both sides. The strangest shopping mecca amid a cultural landscape like a patchwork quilt, something this city had never seen. People coming from all over to shop the ethnic shops in the Market, getting what they couldn't get anyplace else.

Mica saying, "So, you think old Lesham gave credit?"

"My point, those old guys came with nothing, and in spite of it, they made it. And you got to respect that."

"Sure, but do we need to hear it all the time?"

"Maybe you hear the same stories, sometimes stretched out of shape, but nobody ever heard a gripe or moan out of a one of them."

Mica sighed, nodding.

"Hey, not like I don't moan now and then. And I guess you heard, me and Paulina hit a rough patch." Lenny glancing out the shop window.

"She decked you, right?" Mica looking at his bruised face.

"Not the way you think. Look, I'm saying we got to be like them old boys."

"Always did it better. Tougher. Had less and made more. And did it with no English," Mica said. "Ever think those stories got mixed with a bit of baloney?"

"Be careful who you say it to." Lenny looked at the doughy face, the pig eyes blinking behind the glasses. Stopped himself from checking his Omega, the one Paulina gave him for his birthday, the first year they were going out.

"Guess you got a point." Then Mica brightened. "So, what's it going to be, a little nosh, maybe the pastrami?"

"Why not? A half of that, and some brisket, and nice and thin, huh? And give me a tub of that, a medium." Lenny pointing through the deli case.

"Potato salad or the slaw?"

Lenny pointed to the slaw.

Mica saying, "Even if some's been stretched, those old boys had the chutzpah, you got to admit. Guess they still do." Setting the football of pastrami on the slicer, he did a cut, laid it on the waxed paper, holding it up to Lenny.

Nodding, Lenny said, "You want, I'll put a word with Paulina, maybe get the old man helping you out . . ."

"Don't do that, Lenny. I have to do this on my own."

Lenny guessed this was Mica trying to be his own man, not wanting to be beholden to family. Something he might never hear the end of. Watching him slice from the football, and not sure why, Lenny said, "Sure the old man loves you, you know?"

"Who, Isaac? Sure he's the feter, right?" Mica smiled and shook his head like he wasn't so sure. He wrapped the pastrami, then got the brisket.

Lenny stepped back to the shelves, grabbing a pumpernickel, giving it a squeeze, seeing a shadow at the door.

It opened, and the dark-haired guys stepped in. The brothers hanging by the door were Jaco and Carlos, the one in the middle was Luís, guy who socked him in the alley, now stepping past Lenny to the counter, said to Mica, "What's good about it?"

"Pardon?"

"I said what's good. Why should I eat here?"

Lenny stood reading a jar of horseradish, turning enough to watch Jaco and Carlos by the door, forgetting which was which, hearing the conversation at the counter, hoping Luís could act, pull off a Portuguese Brando.

"You're asking the owner what's good?" Mica said, being good-natured about it. "Everything."

"Everything's good, then business is good."

"You want a sandwich?" Mica looked at him, then at the two by the door.

"Ham with butter on both slices, and load on the pickles. And on white bread, not the shingles you people eat."

"Sorry, no ham, and we don't use butter."

"What d'you eat then?" The guy looked at Mica like maybe he was joking.

"Got five kinds of mustard and horseradish, your choice."

"Okay, give me that ..." Pointing to the brisket. "And heap on the mayo."

Mica pointing at a paper sign on the wall: *Don't even ask for mayonnaise.*

"The fuck kind of joint you running?" Luís looked back at the brothers, shaking his head.

Mica started to explain about kashrut, instead saying, "Try the corned beef with the spicy mustard. That's the way I like it."

"The way you like it, huh? Okay, make it three."

"And pickle?" Mica pointed to the case.

Luís looked through the glass. "Yeah, what I said, right?"

"Half or the full sour."

"Building a sandwich, not a rocket." Luís just looked at him, watching Mica get started, saying, "So, business is good, you say?"

"Guess I got no complaints."

"Gonna see about that." Luís nodded back at the brothers.

Mica looked from behind the thick glasses, over at Lenny, corned beef in hand, the slicer whirring behind him.

The brother nearest the door took a jar of dills from a shelf and dropped it, glass shattering, brine and pickles sloshing across the wood floor. Putting on the Portuguese Brando, Luís looked at Lenny, nodding his head toward the door, telling him, "Take a hike, kike."

Lenny shrugged, moved for the door, glad the pork-chop remembered his lines. Took a quick look back, told Mica to have a nice day.

Mica sputtered a protest as the brother by the door closed it behind Lenny.

Stepping to his Galaxie parked out front, Lenny fished in his windbreaker for his keys, opened the passenger door, reached under the driver's seat, put his hand back in his pocket, shutting the door. Looked at his watch again, taking his time, he went back in the deli, whistling that tune, "The Fishin' Hole," the opening number to Andy Griffith, walking between the two brothers and up to the counter.

Frozen, Mica looked like he just wet himself.

"Forgot my meat." Lenny kept a hand in his pocket, bumping past Luís waiting on the sandwiches, saying to Mica, "Ought to get one of those number trees, you know the kind?" Then looked at Luís next to him, saying, "I was here first, in case you didn't notice."

"Should'a kept going when you had the chance."

The two brothers closed in behind him.

Unconcerned, Lenny said, "Mica, keep the slicer going, will ya?" Looking at the man next to him.

Mica stood frozen, the scene unfolding in front of him, looking like his bowels were going to dance the Niagara.

"You gonna shake somebody down, you got to find out a few truths." Lenny sounding sure of himself, ignoring the two behind him.

"That right?" Luís's brows inched together, and he looked at his buddies and said something that wasn't English. "Looks like three to one and a half to me."

The brothers grinned, one saying something to the other, both looking ready to jump.

"You come in a nice place mouthing off, how about you do it in English, show a little class." Lenny looked at the guy, saying, "In fact, let me give you a lesson." Lenny flashed the .32 from his pocket, grabbed hold of Luís's belt, kept him from pulling away, and ground the barrel into his crotch. "This here's a G-U-N gun. Can you say it?"

Luís tried to pull away, looking surprised, not something that was in the script.

"G-U-fucking-N. Say it."

"You fucking crazy." Luís squirmed, Lenny turning him so he had a line on the brothers. "Say it!" Twisting the barrel.

"Ahhhh!" Luís tried to grab at Lenny's hand, but Lenny shoved the barrel, causing more pain.

"G-U-N. Say it!"

"Ahh . . . G-U— ahhh!"

Lenny swinging Luís one way, then the other, eyes on the other two. "Try again."

"G-U— *oww* — leggo!"

"Now you two." Lenny pressed hard, keeping Luís under control. Nodding when they got it right. Lenny shoving their buddy at them.

Lenny pointed the pistol at their feet, the brothers holding Luís, who was sucking to get his air back, looking up at Lenny, half pain, half pissed off.

"You Portu-guys come back, pin a piece of paper with a phone number to your shirts, next of kin we can call, to come collect you after?"

"That how you got the eye, running that mouth?" Luís had composed himself, saying something to the other two.

The two nodded and started for him. Lenny slapping the pistol against the side of Luís's head, turning on the brothers, their buddy stumbling against the deli case and sliding to the floor. Lenny keeping the barrel on them. Not exactly the way he had laid it out, but he owed Luís for blindsiding him in the alley.

"*Jesus Cristo!*" The brother on the left crossed himself, looking at Luís on the floor.

"Not gonna find him in no deli," Lenny said. "And no ham or butter, and no mayo. Now get your buddy and get the fuck out."

They stooped to the fallen man. Carlos saying, "Maybe we come back." Nodding to his brother, then helping Luís up on rubber legs and steering him for the door.

"We'll keep the slicer going," Lenny said, watching them take their man under the arms, dragging him out the door. Lenny looked to a frozen Mica, pocketing the .32, stepping over the brine and busted glass, looking to make sure they left, took a jar of horseradish from the condiment shelf, tossing it and catching it in the air, going to the counter and setting it on top, saying, "So, what do I owe you?" Reaching his wallet from his pants' pocket. Thinking it had gone better than he planned, a nice bit of improv.

"I got to call . . ." Mica going to the wall phone, picking the receiver off the hook, his hand shaking.

"Call who?" Lenny looked at him.

"The c-cops."

"Going to what, tell them I pulled a gun and clobbered some guy, on account he ordered ham, didn't want to wait his turn?"

Mica hung up the receiver, looking at his shaking hand. "They s-said they'd be back."

"Not a chance. The fish learned you got family looking out for you." Lenny thinking yeah, that was smooth, and he was going to look good to Paulina, have her thinking second thoughts about the Get. Nobody going to see what was coming next. Leaning on the counter, he said, "Turn that thing off, will ya? It's giving me a headache."

Mica switched off the slicer, then turned back to Lenny.

"Hey, that the matzo ball?" Lenny pointed at the pot on the warmer.

Mica didn't turn, just said, "What if they got guns?"

"Guess talking about the old guys got me upping my game, you know?" Lenny shrugged. "Now, how about give me a large tub, and you got marble rye?"

Hands still shaking, Mica put the order together, setting the rye, pumpernickel, the tubs of soup and salad on the countertop by the wrapped meats and horseradish. Lenny pointed at the strudel in the case, waited for Mica to box a couple of slices. Then he stepped to the front window, looking out to make sure those guys weren't hanging by his car.

Mica forced a smile, saying, "Today it's on the house."

Lenny feigned surprise, thinking it took an aborted robbery attempt, but he finally got something free in this joint. Watching Mica wrap and bag it all up, handing it over the counter and saying he wouldn't hear of it.

Lenny betting he'd never hear the end of it, along with how he saved her cousin from getting robbed — even if Lenny did set it up. Paying the three guys a hundred each seemed worth every nickel, nobody going to suspect him. And a hell of a lot cheaper than letting Paulina's lawyer take him to the cleaners. Cousin Mica just helped him fix it. Lenny thinking, if that ain't love ...

Then he was thinking of that Righteous Brothers tune, the one about losing that loving feeling, thinking he might stop by Sam the Record Man, buy the 45 and give it to her when he dropped by with the deli. Something for her to play other than that Ipanema number. Knock on her door and say something like, "You don't really get a person till you climb in his skin, walk around in it." A line from a movie she liked. Lenny still acting.

Curling the top of the bag, Mica couldn't thank him enough. Threw in the corned beef sandwiches he had started to make.

Going for the door, thinking this could end up as one of Mica's own stories, one he'd be talking about all his days, maybe giving it a twist where Mica was more than the victim, threatening the pork-chops with the slicer, promising a nice bris if they came back, something like that.

Stopping at the door, Lenny turned, Mica setting the slab of meat back in the case, saying, "Oh, and let's keep this a you-and-me thing. You know Paulina likes to worry."

"Mum's the word." Mica made a gesture with his fingers, zipping his lip.

Lenny opened the door, betting Mica was already reaching the phone, dialing his next of kin before Lenny got the key in the ignition. By day's end it would be the talk around many a supper table. "Pass the kugel, and hey, you hear about Lenny, what he did?" Just what he was counting on.

... *the whipping boys*

Manni Schiller came to the office door, Ernie behind his desk, putting the fix on a race at Fort Erie.

Coughing into his fist, getting Ernie's attention, saying, "Gabe shot two marks he was collecting from." Letting it sink in.

Face reddening, his eyes popping, Ernie jumped from behind his desk, the racing form flying, the chair bouncing off the dented filing cabinet behind him. He couldn't fucking believe it.

Manni filling in the rest: Gabe Zoller arrested for shooting one of the fur guys in the garment district. Shot his secretary too. The guy losing his mind, killing people who owed Ernie money.

Kicking the trash can from behind his desk, paper and garbage scattering across the floor. Ernie grabbed the wood chair by the arms and tried to hurl it, felt the stab in his lower back, the sacroiliac again. Setting it down, he shoved it at the corner on its roller wheels.

Taking a careful step in, Manni stood across from the desk, watching the boss vent, tried to look okay about it, not like he was watching a kid having a fit.

Ernie held his back, wincing. "The man's gone apeshit."

"Looks like that."

"Looks like that, huh?" Ernie said. "The guy's in your crew. He goes off his nut, and you come in here, acting like you got no idea about it."

Dag Malek stepped to the office door, a paper cone of water from the cooler outside, sipping it, taking a temperature read of the situation, Ernie going off like a volcano. More shit likely to get thrown any second. Last month it was the Underwood going out the window, taking a bounce and striking a rum bum sleeping one off in the alley, the ambulance guys carting him off in need of a dozen stitches. A year back Ernie drew the pistol from his drawer, came into the travel office and shot the Tokyo clock off the wall. Telling the cops later he was just cleaning the piece, the damned thing going off, killing a time zone.

"I wanna know what the fuck you're doing about it?" Ernie slapped a hand on the oak desktop, glaring from one to the other.

Manni and Dag glanced at each other. Both knowing better than to say much when Ernie got like this. Manni took a step around the desk and looked out the window, like maybe the answer was out in the laneway. Dag sipped his water, stayed by the door, taking an interest in his shoes.

Scratching at his neck, hard enough to draw blood, Ernie touched the small of his back again, settling down and looking at Dag, saying, "You gonna drink water all day, or you gonna get my chair?"

Taking the paper cup between his teeth, careful not to spill any, Dag stepped over and righted the chair, brushing plaster from the seat. Pushing it behind the desk.

Easing down, Ernie thumped his fist on the desktop. "Here's how this goes. You!" Pointing at Manni. "Get him in here."

Manni saying, "Except he's being held."

Dag swallowed the last mouthful of water, looking for somewhere to toss the coned cup, the trash can on its side, still rocking. Considering whether he should straighten it, deciding to leave it alone.

"Get that fucking shyster to make bail. Then get him in here. Twist, that fucking guy, I'm gonna twist his fucking neck." Pointing at Manni again, the finger saying a lot for a finger. "Make sure he understands, he says word-fucking-one, I mean, word-fucking-one: the cops, the media, his mother, his rabbi, anybody . . ."

"Gabe? Don't got to worry about . . ." Manni seeing his mistake, saying he'd take care of it, looked at Dag, knowing Perry Mason couldn't get Gabe out on bail. Still, Manni was happy to get out of there.

Dag stood with his paper cone. Ernie's nostrils flaring wide, then narrowing, the man pushing his breath in and out, looking around the floor for his racing form. Dag wishing he had more water to swallow.

Ernie looked up at him, like what the fuck do you want?

"Know how a kraut uses a banana like a compass?" Dag not sure why he was telling a joke.

Nothing from Ernie.

"Sets it on top of the Berlin Wall, leaves and comes back later. Side with the bite out of it points east."

Ernie kept staring, fingers drumming on the oak.

Dag tried to sip the empty paper cup, then he got out of there. One thing was clear, Dag wouldn't want to be Gabe "The Twist" Zoller now or any time in the near future — not sure the man even had one.

... *zimmering*

Making the last pick-up, he drove back, took the only parking spot on the block. Lenny walked in the front door of Zimm's Travel, hearing Ernie rant on the phone as soon as he stepped in, something about what he was going to do to that dumb fuck getting arrested for popping the Greek on his route. Just supposed to make his pick-up. Instead he clips the guy, along with his secretary. No pick-up, just bodies. Zoller getting busted a block from the scene, jamming the weapon in the ass end of a chicken. A true fucking moron. The cops bound to come asking questions.

Lenny got all that from hearing Ernie yell. He wondered what was going on, just saw Gabe a couple of hours ago. Sitting at his sales desk under the line of clocks, he felt the breeze from the standing fan, setting the deli bag down and handing the day's pick-ups to Manni, saying, "I'm one light."

"Got to be a full moon." Manni shook his head.

"I'll get it next week, don't sweat it." Lenny knowing how Ernie felt about his collectors coming back light, deciding not to mention the Portuguese stepping into their territory. Not sure how he'd handle it yet, but he'd take care of it, and end up looking good for it after. Asking, "So, what's up with The Twist?"

Manni told him what he knew, adding, "The cops come asking, the guy sold vacations till Ernie canned his crazy ass a week ago. A loose fucking cannon if ever there was."

According to Manni, the cops had a pair of witnesses, two spinster sisters swearing Gabe double-parked them in and went in the building, the sisters hearing gunshots, watching him come out of the Merchant of Mink, getting in his black Catalina and driving off. "Like he brung his own eyewitnesses. Fucker drives off and gets boxed in an alley two blocks from the scene, the cops making the arrest, easy as pie."

Lenny couldn't believe it, asking if Manni was up for some corned beef, offering one of the sandwiches Mica made for the Portuguese.

Ernie was pacing his office in the back corner, kicking his trash can into a wall.

"They connect Zoller to us, gonna set off another investigation, could be we all end up in the same cell block." Manni unwrapped the sandwich, looking up as Ernie came to his door.

"They come with warrants, gonna start seizing and shutting us down," Ernie said, the man with a knack for hearing everything going on inside these walls. A coffee mug in his hand, Zimm's Travel — *come fly with me* in red ink.

"Want a corned beef?" Lenny said.

"I hate corned beef." And Ernie threw the mug against the far wall, an explosion of coffee, bits of ceramic sliding down. Wheeling around, he went back in his office, something else hitting the wall.

"Fucker tried to hide his piece up a chicken's ass, you believe it?" Dag said, shaking his head, then saying, "Hey, Lenny, know how a kraut uses a banana like a compass?"

Ernie called for Dag to get in there.

Dag getting up from behind his desk, said he'd tell him later, going to the boss's office.

Manni sat under the line of clocks showing the current times in Lisbon, Paris, Tokyo, Sydney and New York. Glancing up like he wished he was in any of those other places right about then. Checking off Lenny's entries in a ledger, slipping the cash in a locked drawer, saying, "Waiting to hear from the desk sarge at 92 King." The cop getting an envelope at the start of every month, and worth every penny when something like this went sideways.

Dag stood at Ernie's door, sensing the boss was calming some, daring to say, "You gonna catch a stroke you keep it up."

"Yeah, and maybe I wouldn't mind."

"We'll take care of it, like I said," Dag talking in his easy way, picking up a torn section of newspaper, setting it back on the desk, smoothing it out, hoping to get Ernie's mind back on fixing a horse race.

"Somebody ought to put one in that dumb head."

"The Twist?"

"Who we talking about?"

"You believe he did it, something like that?"

"Since he got plugged, the guy's not been right." Ernie tapping his own temple.

"But still, would he rat?"

"Think he'd sell his mother, he hears the right price."

"Well . . . then you just got to say the word," Dag said.

"What the fuck just came out of my mouth?"

"Wanna be sure, is all."

Ernie giving him a look.

"Okay, then it's done." Turning, Dag went out, grabbing one of Lenny's sandwiches, taking his jacket off the back of his chair, going for the glass door in front. Told Manni he had a call to make. The kind of calls they didn't make from the office, going to use the pay phone up the block.

Then Ernie was yelling again from the office, "Somebody get me that fuckin' ambulance-chaser."

Lifting the receiver, Manni got on the blower to Ross Cohen's office, telling the lawyer's secretary to put Cohen on the line, hearing he was in a meeting, then saying, "Just tell him who it is." Waiting for Cohen to pick up, then telling him to hold the line. He laid the phone down, heard Ernie banging around the office. Waiting for a break before calling, "Got Cohen on one."

"I need coffee." Ernie grabbed the phone and started tearing into the lawyer.

Looking at Manni, Lenny said, "He want it for throwing or drinking?"

"Why don't you go ask him?" Manni reached in his drawer and handed Lenny an envelope — his pay for the week, cash, same as always — then he went to the coffee station by the small fridge, an empty pot on the warmer, Coffee-Mate and a bowl of sugar packets next to it, but no more mugs. Manni went back and sat at his desk, saying, "How about you go fetch him a cup, and I won't mention you came in light."

Lenny tucked away his cash, got up and left the deli bag on the desk and went out the door. Stepping into the early summer heat, Lenny glad to get out of there, wondering what the fuck was happening with Gabe, crossing the street, getting java from the Brazilian joint, tipping the tall girl, Jada, with the dreadlocks, getting that smile. Bringing the take-out cup, something Ernie couldn't break. Tapping on the office door — Ernie on the phone with the lawyer — Lenny set the cup on his desk and got out of there. Grabbing the deli bag and telling Manni he was done for the day.

"Don't want to see how it turns out?"

"Got something to take care of. Call you later." Lenny said, going out the door, getting in the Galaxie and rolling off, hoping the food hadn't spoiled in this heat, making an illegal turn on Spadina, beating an amber, wondering about the shit-storm Gabe got himself in, then he was thinking of his own storm, the one waiting at his own house.

. . . *game plan*

E rnie Zimm held the phone to his ear. The kid lawyer,
Ross Cohen, on the line saying the cops had Gabe
dead to rights on two homicides, explaining that bail was a
fucking fantasy.

"The money I pay you, that's all you got?"

"Like I said, I'll go have a chat in holding. Let him know
you've got his back."

"Not the part of him I wanna hold." Ernie squeezing his
fist, thumping the desk, saying, "He keeps his mouth shut,
you hear me? Or Dag goes and sees his mother in that old
fucks' home. Lights a cigar and tosses it at her oxygen tank.
Make sure he hears it."

"I'll pass it on."

Slamming down the receiver, Ernie stared at the racing
form, blinking his eyes, trying to make the spots go away,
wondering how in fuck a man could concentrate on fixing a
race with all this shit going on.

. . . *blossoms and fish*

Ernie's talk with the lawyer filled the place, Dag Malek tired of hearing the rant, turning as the door to the street opened, thinking Lenny forgot something.

The guy standing there in a fifty-buck jacket with the leather on the elbows, looking around. Dag didn't need to see the badge. Smiling and saying, "I help you, officer?"

The guy smiled back. "It's detective."

"My mistake, detective."

Ernie Zimm was yelling into his phone, "Make sure he hears it." The sound of the receiver hitting the phone cradle.

"I come at a bad time?" the cop said, stepping closer, putting on a smile.

"You practice that, the stand-up routine, acting like you just happened by? More likely sitting in your car, keeping an eye on the place, peeing in your coffee cup."

"I'm a cream-and-sugar man. And sitting outside of this place, naw, I got better things to do."

"That for real, you guys pee in cups?"

"Ones who got good aim. Thing is, we can't take our eyes off all you shit-birds long enough. But, cop or crook, you got to go, you got to go. Am I right?"

"Probably why they call you that, pigs. No offense." Dag smiled at him.

The cop smiled back, hearing a loud crash, nodding to the door in back. "Ernie's getting himself excited, huh?"

"You want to ask questions, then I guess I better see the tin."

"Makes it official, right?" The cop lifted his jacket, the badge clipped to his belt, the holstered pistol showing too, saying he was Gary Evans.

Dag leaned in and made a show of noting the badge number, jotting it on a pad on the desk, then lifted the receiver and pressed a button on the phone. Saying while he waited, "So, I interest you in a well-earned vacation, Detective Evans?"

"I tell you, I wouldn't mind."

The sound of the phone being slammed down in the office.

"The boss could use one too, huh?" Gary Evans smoothed his jacket, starting for the office.

"Mind if I ask what it's about?"

"Like you don't know." The cop smiled.

The office door opened, and Ernie stood with a hand on the threshold. "The man's here in official capacity, Dag. Comes here with his questions, and what's it matter if it's a good time?"

"Yeah, I can ask, and you can hand me a line." Gary Evans smiled at Ernie. "What really matters are the things you boys don't say."

"You got questions, I'm an open book," Ernie said, showing composure, smiling now, holding up a hand, showing him in.

Gary stepped past him and into the office, saying, "Something wrong with your back?"

"Acts up now and then."

"Been seeing this guy, a chiropractor, gave my neck a twist, should've heard the pop. Says it's from all the sitting, keeping places under surveillance, you know. But, I tell you, I walked out of there good as new. Happy to pass along the name and number."

"You guys keep showing up, and going away empty, acting like we're all friends, but I love the attitude." Ernie sat behind his desk. "And thanks for the medical advice."

Gary stood opposite and leaned across, saying, "Heard about you and your fine establishment here, selling tours to the faithful." Gary looking at the racing form on the desk, the trash can on its side, the coffee sprayed against the wall.

"Like the sign says, tours, our specialty. But let me ask you one, this an official call, the kind where you show me papers, the ones that let you come in and poke your nose?"

"Oh, I'm not poking. This one's more a courtesy call."

"So no squad out in my bushes, one of your boys with the ram you all like to use, take the front door off its hinges."

"Nothing like that, but yeah, I love the big black key." Going to the window, Gary Evans had a look out back.

Ernie snapped his fingers, calling out the door. "What do they call them papers, Dag?"

"A warrant."

"A warrant, right. You bring one, deputy? If so, I'll take it to the little room we got in back, give it a read, then put it behind me, you understand what I'm saying."

"You mean wipe your ass with it, yeah, that's a good one. Not the fifth time I've heard it this month."

"So, you got a question, go on and ask it. If not, I got a wife putting on the pot roast."

Gary Evans turned and shut the door, coming back and leaning over the desk, staring into the man's eyes. "I say Gabe Zoller, and you just hand me a line of shit, right?"

"That a question?"

"That's it."

"Could've saved yourself the drive."

"Got your boy walking from a murder scene with two eyewitnesses, the piece he used in the butt of a chicken, caught holding it in his hand. You ask me, it feels like your man Gabe handed us the case. So no, I don't mind making the drive. Gives us a chance to get acquainted."

"Let me save you some time, detective." Dag said coming in.

"Shoot." Gary turned and smiled, keeping them both in view. "A figure of speech, you understand?"

"Can see you got the wrong idea about us," Dag said. "Gabe Zoller wasn't much for selling Miami sunshine, so we had to cut him loose."

"That right?"

"That's right. A week ago. Look, we sell travel, detective. Been satisfying customers nearly twenty years."

"And shaking down the rest."

"Good one," Dag said, "How about this — booked a Mrs. Goldstein a week in Miami Beach, got her a suite at the Fontainebleau. She gets there, goes to the front desk and signs her name, the clerk looks at her signature, tells her she can't stay there. Poor woman goes, 'What do you mean? I paid good money.' Clerk points to a sign saying *NO JEWS*. Our Mrs. G. says, 'I'm no Jew.' 'Course the clerk doesn't buy it, and asks, 'Then who's our Lord?' She gets it right, and he asks where was he born. Again she nails it, throws in the bit about the manger, and the clerk asks, 'Yeah, but why a manger?'

And Mrs. G gets in his face and says, 'Cause a schmuck like you wouldn't rent a room to a nice Jewish couple.'"

Gary Evans smiled, "Yeah, that's a good one." Looking to the door.

Glancing past him to the line of clocks in the outer office, Dag saying, "Let me ask you, detective, maybe Miami's not your scene, but everybody's got a time zone that's close to his heart . . ."

Looking from him, back to Ernie, then at the clocks, Gary Evans smiled and said, "Well, I guess Tokyo's got the blossoms, right? Place where they eat the raw fish. Supposed to be pretty good."

"Yeah, and all them islands," Dag said. "A country enjoying some peace, under the U.S. nuclear umbrella as I understand it. Meaning you can go see the blossoms, eat your fish and not have a care in the world. Word is, they love the sound of Western music over there, the blue jeans, our ways and culture."

"That so, huh?"

"The way I hear it," Dag said.

Gary smiled, looked at Ernie again, then at Dag. "I guess you're giving me something to think about." Couldn't believe he'd just been bribed, Gary Evans went for the door, saying, "Nice to meet you, fellas. Bet we'll be seeing more of each other." The one thing he was sure about.

... *every man a king*

Paulina's Commander Wagonaire sat in the driveway, new model in sienna red. Set Lenny back twenty-seven hundred bucks, and it didn't do a damned thing to improve things between them. Thinking back to when he drove up in it back when he was still living here, and Paulina looked at it in the driveway, and asked, "What's this?"

"Happy birthday, babe." Holding up the keys, he said it was all hers.

Crinkling her nose, saying, "A wagon, huh?"

"Nice and safe. And think of the stuff you can pile in there."

"Like groceries, your dry cleaning?"

Lenny seeing his mistake. Maybe if he'd gone ragtop Malibu, a white one with the red leather interior. Paulina rolling around town with the top down, the breeze blowing her blonde hair. Lenny going for practical, the Studebaker sending the wrong message — like gifting her a washing machine on wheels.

Lining his Galaxie behind it in the drive now, he willed the Ford to crap some oil, have a gasket give up the ghost.

Leave his mark, something that would piss her off. Looking up at the house like he was taking a temperature read. It didn't feel like his place anymore. Her inch-pleat drapes were pulled across the bay window, the new TV tower rising above the re-bricked chimney. The aluminum siding, the eaves replaced, exterior trim painted last year. The flagstones and cedar hedge around the yard. The lawn looking good. Paulina wanting her grass money-green, getting the lawn man to spread on the crabgrass killer, the 3-in-1 lawn food.

He slid the .32 under his car seat, didn't want to hear her going on about why a travel agent had to go around with an unregistered handgun under his jacket, selling Miami cruises. After saving Mica, doing it with the .32, she ought to be okay with it, but why take the chance. Besides, he didn't need the temptation to use it in case things went the wrong way, not shooting her before he was ready.

Lenny had found a receipt for a High Standard derringer she bought, not bothering to discuss it with him first. He called it a double standard and she laughed at him. Didn't matter hers was registered, Lenny wanting to know why the daughter of a jeweler needed a carry permit. Told her she was watching too much *Naked City*. Hearing how a lot of jewelers carried on account of all the crooks out there. Throwing it back at him. But, in back of his mind, he wondered if she had her own ideas about shooting him.

Now he was putting on a show, making nice, bringing a bag of deli. Guessing she heard how he saved her worthless cousin from a robbery or worse. Maybe she'd see him in a better light, maybe the rest of the family would too. Then he'd let Luís and his greasers loose, guys who must have followed him to his house — Paulina getting caught in some kind of revenge — the three of them coming after Lenny for interfering at the deli, the real reason for the show at

Mica's. Lenny going from zero to hero in the family's eyes, not suffering through an ugly divorce, and not suspected of wrongdoing.

He'd play like it was no big deal when she said something about him foiling the robbery, something like, "It's a good thing I felt like brisket, huh?" And a good thing he kept the .32 under the car seat too.

The doorbell chime made the place sound hollow — just barking coming from inside — he juggled the bag of deli, thinking he best get it in the fridge, so goddamn hot outside.

Putting his finger through the hole of the sleeved 45 record he got at Sam's, he spun it, then got out his key and let himself in, thankful she hadn't changed the locks. Didn't smell like cooking when he opened the door, just a hint of Pledge. "The Girl from Ipanema" not playing, Paulina spinning that record to death the past month before he moved out. She'd done the same thing when "Silhouettes" hit the charts, the Herman's Hermits number. And the Beatles' latest, "Ticket to Ride." Telling Lenny, back when things were still working, he ought to grow a mop top, told him combing it the way he did, along with the sideburns, was out.

Her white poodle, Baby, stood at the top of the stairs with its own dumb haircut, looking at him like she was deciding who he was. Maybe she was smiling or was showing her teeth, he couldn't tell. Wouldn't put it past Paulina to turn Baby against him. The dog slow coming down the stairs, sniffing the deli bag, Lenny giving her a pat.

Nothing said "welcome" about the place anymore. Lenny looked around, guessing he might have picked the wrong day to set up the fake robbery. He put the bag on the hall table, where she usually kept a vase of flowers, supposed to make the place feel cheery. Maybe the vase was a casualty, something she smashed against the wall the last time he was here.

He'd tell her he should have called first, but didn't want to talk about the thing at Mica's over the phone, expecting she had caught the gossip through the club's yenta telegraph, or more likely from Mica himself. Showing she had him wrong all along. A gangster with a loving side and a good heart.

With her car in the drive, she could be napping off one of those icepick headaches plaguing her since the marriage went south. Going to the bottom of the stairs, he called up.

Nothing.

Could be next door at Swoozie's for cocktail hour, meaning the whole block knew their marriage was kaput. He went to the side door leading to the garage and closed it behind him, turned on the bare bulb over the workbench and got the old can from behind the line of paint cans, looked for the rainy-day cash he kept tucked inside. Damn thing was empty.

"Fuck me."

Meaning Paulina had found it. He went back in the house. Baby by the counter, sniffing up at the deli bag.

"Yeah, you wish," he told her, thinking of sitting in his old armchair, in front of the boob tube, let Irv Weinstein bring him the news from across the lake in Buffalo. And later, Les Crane or Johnny Carson. Wait till she got home, pissed off seeing him sitting there with his feet up. Then he'd ask her, "Where is it?" Then, "You know what money."

He went to the kitchen and took the phone off the cradle, calling Zimm's, talking to Dag Malek.

Ernie was still ranting in the background. Dag saying they were still waiting on word about Gabe, the two of them knowing better than to talk business on the phone. From next door, he heard Swoozie's yard man crank up the lawn mower. Not having much luck from the sound of it.

If Paulina wasn't next door, then she could be at the club, or maybe she took a walk over to her old man's house, about a half mile away. The princess wanting to live close to her folks. Lenny playing along at the time and taking on a mortgage on this place that could choke a rhino, this house on the skirt of Lawrence Park. No way he could convince her to pick a new place for less money in the suburbs, Etobicoke or North York. She insisted on staying close to family.

He never had much use for her folks, especially the old man, and he knew the feeling ran mutual, and it ran deep. Old Isaac Levine coming over to break bread, always sitting opposite Lenny, acting like his end was the head of the table. Lenny sick of people talking how it was a miracle the old man survived the death camps over twenty years back. The son of a bitch looking across the table at Lenny like he was thinking, no way you would have made it.

And Paulina's mother, Helen, that woman could smile ice chips as she passed the latkes. Been gone to cancer two years now. Lenny not surprised, all that bitter misery, and lately seeing how Paulina was turning more into her mother with every passing day.

Switching on the TV, letting it warm up, from white dot to fade-in, he went to the kitchen and grabbed the deli bag, fixing a brisket on marble rye, spreading on the horseradish. The poodle drooling twin lines at the threshold, watching him fix the sandwich. Lenny tossed her a slice, knowing she got the trots every time she ate anything that didn't say Purina on it, Lenny thinking it would give Paulina something to do later. He tossed some brisket, the dog snapping it from the air like Yogi Berra.

He switched the channel to *Bewitched*. Imagining Paulina going from Samantha to Endora, been happening since the day he stomped his heel on that fucking glass.

He hadn't gone sniffing around yet, but there was no shortage of knish on the street — the whole town with neon signs flashing *girls, girls, girls*. There was Jada, working at the Brazilian place where he got the coffee, across from Ernie's agency. Jada flirting with him, telling him her name meant God's gift, saying it in that accent. Lenny saying he believed it. And there was the free-love divorcée, Marilynn, who told him she was lonely up in Yorkville, Lenny booking her a Florida cruise last month, flirting with her to make the sale. Peroxide hair piled up, a full figure and a Wonderbra pressing up her goodies. Thought about that as he dished himself some slaw.

Paulina had blamed his world of secrets. Told him she was done with it, and he was free to do whatever and whoever he wanted, pretty sure he'd been doing it since they got hitched. She wanted him out, and told him she wanted a Get, a rabbi's blessing for separation, Lenny knowing it would be followed by a bloodletting divorce.

"You want out, and I'm supposed to take care of it, huh?"

"It's how it works, Lenny. It's what you signed up for. Be a man for once." Paulina keeping with traditions, Lenny betting she was doing it for the old man. A guy who never had any use for him.

"That's what you want — out?" A figure of speech, but not the only figure she was after, he was sure of it.

"I want you out, Lenny. That's all."

She intended to clean him out and leave him hanging, maybe literally. Lenny on the hook with Ungerman, owing a hundred Gs on the apartment block, and with Gabe in the can charged with murder, maybe he'd be on the hook for all of it.

Last time they talked, Lenny let loose, "You think you're taking my house? Think again."

Paulina throwing the marble ashtray, five pounds of wedding gift. Knocked plaster from the wall next to his head, the dust falling and the lath showing through. Baby yelping and running up the stairs, Lenny walking out as she flung the pinwheel crystal from the dining hutch, half the set exploding like shrapnel against the wall by the time he slammed the front door behind him.

The next time they spoke was on the phone, Lenny calling from the Empress at Yonge and Gould, the room he rented on the third floor, paying a week at a time.

He had told her it was in her best interest, think of him as working in the travel business. Paulina bothered by the "hush" around his work since day one, knowing who Ernie Zimm was and what the outfit was into. Told him half the folks at synagogue knew what he did too, Paulina dying of embarrassment. Lenny saying she knew he was in the life when she met him, the thing that put this roof over their heads, the living-room set from Eaton's, the Zenith and Frigidaire from the Bay, the turquoise matching the cooktop and the wall oven. And the Studebaker wagon in the driveway, every option known to man: the bucket seats, sliding roof, Daytona trim and overdrive. Paulina playing tennis and hanging around that club where the women played too little and talked too much. Paulina complaining the girls at the club knew all about Ernie Zimm's Travel, a tax-dodging front for crooks. Maybe at one time she thought she could change Lenny, admitting she'd been blinded by his fake success, at least at first.

Took a bite of the brisket when he heard footsteps on the stoop, the front door opening. Baby forgetting she was mooching cold cuts and ran, feet sliding on the tiles, her marshmallow tail wagging.

Paulina coming in, patting Baby's head, looking at him in the kitchen, the TV on, saying, "Oh, Lenny . . ."

Not happy to see him, and not alone. The shadow of a man behind her on the stoop. Paulina turning and saying, "You mind giving me a minute?" Calling him Gary.

This Gary was about Lenny's height, had a few pounds on top of a one-time athletic build, dark hair combed fifties style, even more out of style than Lenny's.

"Yeah, I'll be right here." Said he'd be by the car, turning and going down the steps.

She looked back at Lenny, waiting for an explanation.

"New friend?" Lenny said.

Paulina closed the door behind her and stepped in. Lenny thinking it was the same outfit she was in this morning, when he was spying from across the park. His ex-wife wearing eye shadow and lipstick, and if she took a step closer, he bet he'd catch the Chanel too.

"Why're you here, Lenny?" Patting Baby's head, her cold eyes on him.

"Tried calling first." He pointed to the bag on the kitchen counter. "Thought you might be up for some deli. Stopped by Mica's, told me you'd been in." Hoping she heard the rest of it.

"So I guess you heard I already had deli. Why'd I want it again?"

He shrugged.

"And you can see I've got company."

"A date?"

Paulina stood on the rug, those eyes not looking at him the way they used to. Patting the dog's head, she said, "Tell me you didn't give her any?"

"Think I'd know better by now, huh?"

"You bring the Get?"

"Just the brisket."

"So, why?"

"Don't like how we ended last time, you throwing all that stuff — the heat of the moment."

"I just want out of this, Lenny, this you and me."

"Careful what you ask for." He set the half-eaten sandwich on the plate, his appetite gone.

"That thing at Mica's, yeah, I heard. That why you're here?" Paulina opened the door, saying, "It's too late for that, Lenny."

"I told Mica not to say anything."

"It's nice what you did, I guess, but what does it change?"

"You think I risked my life to impress you? Come on, Paulie, give yourself a jiggle."

"A jiggle? That's subtle, Lenny."

"Think you ought to see somebody. And I don't mean a cop."

"A what?" Giving him incredulous.

"That guy." Lenny nodded at the door, meaning the guy she came with.

"Wrong again. He teaches science — the tenth grade."

"More like second-grade detective."

"Oh, another guy I'm seeing, he's a lawyer."

"Yeah? He know about you two?" Lenny got up and went to the bay window, looking at the guy down by his car, leaning against it, checking out Lenny's car, then glancing around the neighborhood, taking in the details. A cop, no doubt about it.

"I'm seeing the lawyer about the divorce," she said.

"Yeah, ask if he knows a good shrink." Lenny getting pissed, her treating him like this after he supposedly saved her spineless cousin.

"Want to know what he said?"

"Who?"

"The lawyer."

"Rather hear about your friend there." Lenny was wondering about the cop, likely seeing her to get to him, mining for information.

"Ought to get yourself one too, a lawyer."

A thin smile, and he said, "You and this lawyer think we're dividing everything down the middle, huh?" Everything he'd worked for, risked his neck while she wore tennis whites and played singles at the club. Lenny seeing himself taking a chainsaw down the middle of the goddamn loveseat, the TV, the bed, that fucking Wagonaire — everything he'd paid for.

"I don't want half, Lenny," she said. "Not after what you put me through."

"This the real you coming out, huh?"

"Lenny, understand this, I'm not out to hurt you."

"Got a funny way of showing it." The woman had no idea about hurt, or what he could do.

"Well, maybe I want you to feel something . . ." Crinkling her nose. "Just a little."

"I got that when you were throwing all the glassware." Lenny getting a clear picture of which side of their assets she was thinking. Both sides.

"I should've known better, no doubt," she said. "So I'll take some of the blame."

"Along with the house and everything in it."

"They're just things, Lenny. It's not what counts."

Lenny took the sandwich from the plate and tossed it to the dog.

Baby caught it and chomped it down, three big gulps.

"I gave up two years to your lies, so it's as down the middle as this gets. Oh, and I took the cash from your little rainy-day fund you didn't think I knew about — the lawyer needed a retainer."

"Real cute."

"What you won't get, Lenny, you won't get me talking."

"Like to the cop?" The gloves were off now. Lenny feeling the rage kicking inside.

"Keep it up, and I won't even feel sorry when I'm doing it." Then she went to the door, opened and held it. "You come back, bring the Get. You'll be free, see anybody you want and take her on that cruise you always talked about."

Lenny stepped to the door, face to face with her, saying, "You know the people I work for, Paulie. They even think you're talking to a cop . . ."

"You don't scare me, Lenny. Go hang in the shadows. I don't care. Just sign the papers, and let me get on with my life."

Lenny stepped out of there, thinking what Ernie Zimm would do if he found out she was talking to a cop, or even to a lawyer, telling them her husband was a gangster. No way that was going to happen.

The cop stood leaning against his passenger door, looking at him. Lenny thinking maybe he'd be the one responding to the call, find her in the back of her Studebaker, pushed off the Scarborough Bluffs some night. And if Ernie saw the whole mess as Lenny's fault, marrying a woman like that, not keeping his house in order and jeopardizing the operation, could be Lenny would end up in the back of the wagon next to her.

She called after him, "Oh, just so you know, I wrote a statement and gave it to my lawyer."

That stopped him; he turned and looked at her. Who was this woman? Saying, "Yeah, your lawyer got a name?" Couldn't be one from this town, not one who knew the name Ernie

Zimm; the Zimm who bought jurors, harassed witnesses, had people tamper with evidence. Handing envelopes to cops, judges and city officials.

Lenny got to his car, looking at the cop standing against his own car, looking back. Lenny got in, rolled down the passenger window and backed out, leaning across and saying, "Got her all warmed up for you, officer. Careful, she tickles easy." And he drove out of there.

And he was thinking of getting one of the furriers they collected from, one that Gabe hadn't shot, turn that poodle into a stole and give it to her for her next birthday. Except she wouldn't be around that long. Lenny remembering the bag of deli on the counter, hoping she choked on it. The woman going from wife to cunt badger, spreading her legs for some cop, thinking she was keeping the house and everything in it.

Gripping the wheel, he stopped at a light, glaring at the son-of-a-bitch red light. Stomping his foot, laying a patch and blasting through the light. Yelling, "Fuck you!" to the red light.

And he sped along Lawrence, east of the Don, before he thought about where he was going. Cranking the wheel and turning and heading back to the Empress, another night of lice and a stained mattress. Kicking the throttle, he played out the scene, what had to be done. There would be no Get and no lawyers. She wanted out, okay, she was going to be out.

. . . raincheck

"Everything okay?" Gary Evans asked her, recognizing Lenny from the photo in the case file. Gary wanting to go after him and drag him out of his car, but not how a science teacher would do it.

It had been Paulina's idea, asking him back for a nightcap. The two of them getting to know each other, feeling more like a date than just lunch after a match. The two of them spending half the afternoon lingering over coffee.

No denying she had his pulse kicking. Gary feeling guilty with thoughts of climbing into bed with the ex-wife of the dirtbag he was trying to take down. Thinking how he'd handle it, turn his head on the pillow and say, "By the way, I'm not really into science. Fact, I used to fall asleep in class." And now he could see the truth coming straight at him like a rushing freight.

"I told you about my split, right?" Paulina said.

"Called him your ex. That's him, huh?"

"I guess we're at the messy part."

"You want to talk, I'm good at listening, but if you want to take a raincheck . . ."

"If you don't mind." A headache like a thunderclap building behind her glassy eyes.

"A raincheck it is." Not how he really felt, but Gary put on a smile, patting the poodle's head, asking its name, standing awkward at her door. As far as it was going tonight. Keeping the smile, he said, "Guess I'll see you at the club."

"Glad you understand, Gar—"

And he leaned in for a kiss.

Paulina turning her head, his lips brushing her cheek.

She said, "Sorry."

It was time to go, Gary going for the steps, Baby retching up a spray of vomit. Gary looking down at the yarked brisket inside his cuffs and across his shoes. Little bits of meat.

Her hand went to her open mouth, Paulina saying, "Oh my, I'm really sorry, Gary."

"No sweat. I got this dry cleaner right down the street." Somehow he kept the dumb smile, saying it like dogs threw up on him all the time. Going down the driveway, trying to keep some dignity, not walking like he felt the puke soaking his pant leg. Gary wondering if there was going to be a next time. Yeah, he'd lied to her, and there was no way around that, so he guessed he deserved what he got. If nothing else, he would do one thing for her, put Lenny Ovitz behind bars and let her get on with her life without a guy like that in it.

. . . sweatbox

G abe Zoller looked at his wrist handcuffed to the table leg, thinking his fingers were turning blue. These sadistic fucks cranking them too tight. Shifting one cheek for the other, his ass sore from sitting on the wooden chair in this tiny room where they interrogated the perps. Running a finger over carved initials, CM, in the wood top, Gabe wondered how a collar snuck something sharp into interrogation, leaving his mark under the watch of the cops.

The detective who'd come in called himself Gary Evans, went for friendly with his James Drury looks, dressed in no-style casual, slacks and a sweat top, grilling him with smiling questions.

Getting nowhere, Evans sent the uniform at the door down the hall for food and coffee, the tall cop coming back and tossing a wrapped sandwich on the table, a cheese slice with onion and butter between two slices of Wonder. A paper cup of something dishwater-brown. The detective acting like he was doing Gabe a favor, watching him unwrap the sandwich with his free hand. Taking a bite, Gabe chewed and tossed the sandwich on the table, spitting the mouthful into the cup, liquid spilling — Gabe pushing it away.

"Not to your liking?"

"Maybe good the year they made it."

Gary told him the old guy servicing the vending machine only came on Wednesdays, then said, "You say something interesting, maybe I'll send for take-out."

"My lawyer can bring me a slice."

"The lawyer Ernie Zimm's taking his time sending?"

"You got a smoke? Always a nice finish to any meal."

Gary pulled a pack from a pocket, offered a Player's non-filtered and took out his lighter.

Gabe puffed it to life using his free hand and took a long drag. Said, "At least *it's* fresh."

"I meet guys like you, ones who figure they'd get away with shit, you know, acting like the world owes them a living. Anyway, some of them were half-smart, could have taken up a trade, made something of themselves. Then there's guys like you."

"You think I'm dumb?" Gabe took a long drag.

"You double-parked in front of the eyewitnesses. Shoved the murder weapon in a chicken. Now sitting here acting like you're going to walk. What do you think I think?"

"Maybe the chicken did it." Gabe flicked ash on the Wonder Bread.

"Breakfast's at seven, continental from what I understand." Gary Evans got up for the door, banging for the uniform to open it. "Meantime, hope Ernie's lawyer shows up with your slice, otherwise get set for a long night."

When he was gone, Gabe smoked the cigarette down and stabbed the butt into the bread a couple of times. His ass hurt more as time passed, moving his weight from cheek to cheek, the uniform finally coming back in and unhooking his wrist from the table leg and leading him back to the holding cell. A passed-out drunk curled on one of the bunks, doing a nasal recital, a urine reek coming off the other bunk, filling the place.

Sitting on the floor with his back against the wall, finally lying down and curling on the floor before O'Riordan, the desk sergeant, came through the outer door, taking his ring of keys and his time selecting the right one. The sarge looked at the drunk on the other bunk, like he was deciding if the smelly guy was still alive.

"My lawyer here?"

The sarge looked at Gabe like he hadn't noticed him, took the ring of keys in his fist, saying, "Give me a reason, I'm beggin' you, fuck-o." Opening the cell door, he motioned him up, led him back down the hall and shoved Gabe back into the interrogation room. Stepping behind him, the sarge dug his thumbs into Gabe's collarbones, pushing him into the wooden chair and cuffing his wrist back to the same table leg. Laughing as he left Gabe to stare at the walls, picking a fingernail at the carved initials in the table.

Twenty minutes before the pain left his neck, and one of the arresting cops came in, the one who'd kicked the chicken and watched Gabe's piece fall out. Followed by a pudgy guy looking like the shorter half of Simon & Garfunkel, decked in a discount suit that looked like he was hoping to fit into it some day. Gabe's first thought was Ernie Zimm was going cheap on legal representation — the man pissed at Gabe on account of the two misses, plus capping the Merchant of Mink.

The cop left and the guy in the cheap suit sat, setting his vinyl briefcase on the floor. The usual deal was the uniform would stand outside the door, let them talk so the lawyer could lay it out, ask if Gabe said anything to the arresting cops, explaining how everything they discussed was privileged. And Gabe would hear him out, how this case was heading for some superior trial court, how the little lawyer had to apply for a release hearing, hoping to get Gabe kicked on bail, *yadda yadda*.

Gabe had been around the block and knew how this worked. No way he wanted to be held until the hearing, but knowing while he was stuck inside, Ernie Zimm would have Dag and Manni beating the bushes, talking to their department sources, finding out about the witnesses, who they were, where they lived. Within a night or two there'd be a knock at their door, the two sisters getting convinced it was in their best interests to have seen no evil, heard no evil, and above all to speak about no evil. Eyewitnesses made to understand that testifying in court ought to come with a health-hazard warning, like the ones they were putting on cigarette packs in the U.S. Whatever the sisters had seen would become clouded by amnesia, a serious case of doubt growing in their minds. And they'd tell the Crown attorney they were sorry, how they made a mistake. Gabe "The Twist" Zoller just wasn't the guy.

Cheap Suit started talking, "Mr. Zoller, I'm Terrence Dow, Crown attorney working your case. Terry to my friends." Meaning he was on the wrong team, which explained the off-the-rack poly suit, and the cop standing outside the door, glancing in the tiny window.

Gabe leaned back, waiting for it.

"I was hoping to have a word."

"I'm all ears." Gabe rattled the bracelet.

Dow shrugged, reached and set the briefcase on the table, working the clasps.

"Where's my guy, the one I'm supposed to talk to?"

"You tell me." Dow shrugged and looked around the room, saying, "I understand you made your call after booking. That right?"

"You know I did and probably know I had a piss an hour ago."

"Sure your counsel will explain when he shows. Let's hope before you need to go pee again."

"'Less you're playing some game?"

"I don't have time for games, Mr. Zoller. Too many wolves acting like lambs. Hey, you mind if I call you Gabe?"

"Tell you what, how about you save the act? You and my guy can talk all the legal horseshit you want."

"Well, since you and I are here, maybe I can save you some time." Dow took out a manilla folder.

"I'm in no rush."

"Meaning you like it here, getting used to the digs?" Dow glanced around the gray walls like he was considering the decor, then at Gabe leaning on account of the cuffs.

"Feels like home, yeah. Concrete walls, a smell of a bladder turned inside out, like when I put Momma in the home." Gabe lifting his arm and jiggling the cuffs.

"Well, I bet she's a proud momma. But, since I'm here, let's discuss your options."

"That include me walking out of here?"

"Can't tell if you're being funny, Gabe," Terrence Dow said, opening the folder, glancing at a couple of pages. "Don't know you that well yet."

"I'm a laugh a minute, 'specially after a night like I had. How about your boy there loosens the cuffs and lets back some circulation?"

"What have you got to trade?" Terrence Dow looked serious.

"For circulation? How about I won't sue you?"

"That's good." Dow smiled and looked over the papers, making *tsk tsk* sounds and frowning.

Gabe leaned back as far as the cuffs allowed, bored with the show.

Terrence Dow read in silence, then looked up and folded his hands on the papers.

"Somebody said something about food coming," Gabe said.

"Ah, the continental." Terrence Dow nodded and turned to the officer outside the small window in the door, made a hand gesture, and the cop disappeared. Then he took a pen and legal pad from his case and set them down and slid them across, saying, "Tell me in your own words, Gabe."

"The cops grabbed me, stuck a gun in my chicken and wrecked my supper, dragged me down here, saying I shot somebody. Locked me up — total bullshit." Gabe slid the papers back.

"That how you want to play it?"

"Some dick comes in in a cheap outfit like yours, starts asking me questions, giving me stale on white, and fucking coffee like Drano." Gabe glanced at the pathetic excuse for a sandwich still on the table, a fly buzzing around the cigarette butt stabbed into the middle, preferring it to the bread and slice of cheese. The spilled coffee nearly dried now.

"Ah, the vending machine," Terrence Dow said. "Yeah, a shame the guy just comes Wednesdays."

"Like poison on white."

Picking up a sheet of paper from his case, Terrence Dow said, "I read the report, Gabe. Asked to make my assessment, looking at the likelihood of conviction. And I'm not seeing it, the bullshit part. Tell you the truth, I'm seeing a walk in the park, a slam dunk putting you away." Giving another smile.

"Let's see what my guy says."

"I'm looking forward to it." Terrence Dow rose from his chair, saying, "Meantime, you're being charged with second-degree murder in the death of Cyd Doukas and Dimitra Angelos." Said it casual, like he was talking about the weather.

"Don't know any Cyd or Angelo, and fuck you, I got nothing else to say."

"But you do wish representation?"

"Told you I made my call."

"To Ernest Zimm."

"That's right."

"So you're in the employ of Mr. Zimm?" Terrence Dow took the pen and made a note on the pad.

"Go fuck yourself."

Dow looked thoughtful and tapped his pen on the pad, finally said, "Sure you understand the seriousness of the charges, Gabe?"

"How about you stop talking like I'm a moron."

"You're kinda making that part easy."

Gabe shook his head.

"Two eyewitnesses put you leaving the Merchant of Mink after shots were fired. Both picked you out, didn't take them ten seconds."

"Picked me from your nose. You assholes didn't even do a line-up."

"You're in the book, Gabe — a regular celebrity. Profile and straight on, and they made you easy, both pointing to your mug shot. According to the statements, not a shadow of doubt."

"Yeah well, guess we'll see." Gabe leaned back, knowing it would never stick.

"The lab team dusted the scene, doing a full crime lab. I

understand they'll have results by the time your continental breakfast shows up."

"Fuck you."

"You touch anything in that place, Gabe? A doorknob, a wall, the water cooler, anything?"

"This place I never been."

"Until the evidence says different."

Gabe thought he wouldn't mind reaching across the desk and taking a swipe at this smug little prick.

The uniform stepped back in, leaned close to Dow and whispered something, his eyes on Gabe.

Dow nodded and thanked the cop, waited until the metal door shut again, then looked back at Gabe.

"My lawyer here?"

"Want to tell me about the beating at the Market, Gabe?" Dow said. "Happened just ahead of the shooting. That what set you off?"

"You guys don't quit."

"The victim, along with a witness, both pointed at you, even knew your name. Put you walking out of there, holding a chicken by the neck and getting in your ride out front."

"Another frame-up."

"Uniforms did some canvassing, a couple more locals say you've been shaking down the whole block. All ready to swear it under oath."

Gabe looked bored.

"The same chicken you used as a holster, the pistol in the double homicide."

"Like I said, go ask the bird."

"No doubt the casings and your prints'll match up too."

Gabe ran his free hand over his forehead, looked at the dead sandwich, saying, "One bite and now I'm feeling the trots coming on. So, if you don't mind ..."

Terrence Dow leaned back and steepled his fingers on the pad of paper, smiling as he said, "Here comes the best part, Gabe."

"When you watch me shit my pants?"

"When the realization clicks in, the perp seeing there's no place to run. What I call the gotcha moment." Dow smiled.

"I was never there, in them places. Now, you gonna get your goon to walk me back to the can? 'Cause in a minute you gonna see what 'no place to run' looks like."

"Signed statements from two eyewitnesses, the discharged murder weapon, plus the slugs and prints." Dow tapped the pen. "Not to mention the assault beforehand, more statements and witnesses. I could give this case to my six-year-old."

"After I visit the can, I wanna make my call again. You deny it, and I'm gonna talk to the media."

"I'm going to let you use the toilet, Gabe, then you can make another call. Meantime, I'll see about you getting breakfast. And, Gabe, if you got any sense, maybe think about hearing me out."

"I told you, when my guy gets here." Gabe felt his bowels churning, thinking the bull put something on that sandwich. All it took was one bite. Wouldn't put it past these guys.

"Well, it's up to you," Dow said. "Thought you'd want to hear how I can shave off some of the twenty-five-to-life you're staring at." Dow looked at him, and there it was, that hesitation in the eyes, the gotcha moment. Putting the pad and papers back in his case, he smiled as he got up and went and knocked on the door.

. . . *the wind-up*

"You guys are supposed to be pros, right?" Lenny said, sliding into the booth of the Lisbon Club, something called fado playing on the Seeburg, the .38 in his jacket pocket. Looking across the table, Luís and the brothers looking like they wanted to take turns holding his beating heart. "First off, you walk in Sergio's, and tell him he's gonna pay you now. Middle of Ernie Zimm's turf." His eyes were adjusting to the dim. The smell of sardines frying in the kitchen in back. What looked like a line of daytime regulars along the bar, some speaking Portuguese, all watching the replay of the World Cup qualifying match against Romania, drinking glasses of Heineken and Mateus, this place dark like a cavern.

He looked to Luís, the one he'd clapped with his pistol, telling him he was just squaring things for the sucker punch out back of Sergio's. "I didn't do it, there'd be no respect. Now we got an understanding between us." Leaning back, saying, "So, what are we drinking?"

Luís Maria da Silva pointed to his temple, the bandage pad over a red welt. Anger behind his yellowed eyes. Saying, "Only hurts when I blink."

"Yeah, I know the feeling." Lenny winked his bruised eye, looked from Luís to Jaco Leão, saying to him, "Make it a brandy sour. Bet they got that here, huh?"

Staring and waiting until the man slid from the booth and went to the bar. Lenny feeling the hairs go up on the back of his neck as the man passed behind his seat. Going and speaking Portuguese to the bartender.

Turning back to Luís, Lenny said, "What's the one thing I said?"

Luís looked amused at the third man, Carlos, Jaco's brother, saying, "You believe this guy?" Then back to Lenny. "You walk in here, maybe you start thinking if you're gonna walk out."

"I asked you, what's the one thing?"

"Supposed to lean on the guy, you step up and we back off, make you look good. How we did it, till you went Tarzan of the Apes. Man, you got some culhões coming in here, you know it?" Cupping his hands like he was holding vine-ripened beefsteaks.

Lenny nodded like yeah, he knew it.

"But, maybe no brains."

"All I said was to make it look real. All you had to do."

"Yeah, shake him up, give him the stink-eye, show him the blade. You not see his little Jew hands shake like a girl?" Carlos said.

"I didn't buy it," Lenny said, unimpressed. "Why I had to ad-lib."

Luís pointed at his temple. "My head's like an eggplant, and you don't buy it."

"Didn't get it right, I don't know . . . missing the panache, you know?" Not sure why, but Lenny was having fun, looking at these two, glancing over at Jaco at the bar, his back to the table, trading hushed words with the bartender.

The bartender shook his head, Jaco taking him by the forearm, the bartender looking this way, then shook off Jaco's hand, nodding and going about the business of fixing a drink.

Lenny saying, "Tell you what, give you an extra twenty for your pain." Reaching in a pocket, pulling out a roll of bills, thumbing one off, sliding it across. "Get yourself some Aspirin."

"You're pretty close to getting dragged out back for real this time." Luís leaned back in the seat, didn't even look at the twenty.

Jaco came back and slid a sweating glass across to Lenny, walked behind him, slid in the booth, picking up his own glass, saying, "Saude." Looking at Lenny.

"L'chaim ..." Lenny palmed the glass, lifted it, looking at Jaco, the man watching him do it. Lenny set it back down without sipping, saying, "You guys too busy acting like you got the ... what'd you call 'em?"

"Culhões" Carlos said.

"Right."

"What're you saying?" Carlos asked, narrowing his eyes, like maybe he'd been insulted and somehow missed it.

"I'm saying we forget all that, put it behind us." Looking at the drink, then over at the man behind the bar, another greaser looking this way.

"Man's not happy with the job we did," Luís said to Jaco.

Jaco said something Lenny didn't understand, the brothers glaring at him.

"Yeah, I didn't buy it." Lenny was shaking his head again. "Should be asking for my money back. Think maybe I'll get the Jamaicans."

"I'm putting ice from my drink on my head ..." Luís pointed to the ugly bruise changing color under the bandage.

"You're talking about getting money back and hiring the bumbaclots."

"How about we just cut to it?" Carlos pulled a straight razor from a pocket, unfolded it, letting Lenny have a look. "Maybe time you meet navalha."

"That your girlfriend?" Lenny looked at him, this guy forgetting about the pistol in Lenny's pocket, the guy not too bright. But that's what he needed, guys on the low rungs of the ladder, just getting past homo erectus. Then Lenny made like he was conceding, no big deal, saying, "Look, fellas, it ended up my man bought it — just enough, you understand — and I guess that's close to enough." Lenny looked from one to the other, then said, "The only reason we're still talking."

The three of them looked at each other, then turned back to Lenny.

Luís saying, "A lot of words coming out, but you don't say much."

Lenny looked at the two brothers, his hand in his pocket, taking his time getting to the point. "Don't know what the fuck you two were doing, one looking like the doorman, the other like the valet." Lenny frowned at the razor in the hand, then at Carlos who held it. "Think you scare me? You don't scare me. But you wanna try your luck, go ahead." Leaning back and waiting, saying, "Be a shame to shoot a hole in a good jacket."

Carlos ran his thumb across the blade, staring back.

Lenny with his hand in the pocket, feeling the trigger.

Luís put out a hand, touching Carlos's wrist, and said something that got the man leaning back, putting the blade away, the man still eye-fucking Lenny.

Lenny saying to Luís, "I got something else, and I'm thinking this time it's a one-man job. Guess you'll do. You can leave these two at home. That is, if you're up for it."

Luís snapped his fingers, saying, "I snap again and they cut."

"Yeah, they that fast, huh? Do it before I pull the trigger." Lenny taking the .32 from his jacket, setting the butt on the edge of the table. "Maybe someday I'd like to see it, but right now, we got business." And he waited.

"Finish your drink," Jaco said, looking at the glass in front of Lenny. "Then get the fuck out."

"And go to the Jamaicans, the guys who'll do it right." Lenny was getting tired of the bullshit now, but he waited.

"Maybe I heard of this Zimm. But, I never heard of you." Luís said and nodded to the brothers, both leaning back, arms over the back of the bench.

Lenny reached in his other pocket and thumped a roll of cash on the table, an elastic around it. He kept his hand on it.

Carlos saying something to Luís in Portuguese.

"Let's hear about this job," Luís said. "Another show?"

"The kind of show where nobody's around to give you a review." Lenny telling them it was a jewelry store.

Luís nodded, saying, "Ernie Zimm know about it?"

Lenny looked at him and said, "Place I'm talking about's uptown, where Ernie Zimm's got no business. Just a woman behind the counter."

"Something to do with the deli?"

"It's five bills for your troubles," Lenny said.

Luís shrugged and reached for the roll, tucking it away, saying, "You want a woman gone, it's five each man."

"Like I said, I only need one."

"One for the job, two for the wheel, and three for the alibi." Lenny looked at these guys shaking him down.

"And you get the gun, a clean one," Luís said.

Lenny gave it another moment, looking over at the futebol on the TV everybody else in the place was watching, saying, "You know how it ends up, right?"

Luís smiled, saying, "Two to one. I think it's our year."

"Salud." Lenny started to pick up the glass, looked at it, then at each man in turn, and he set it back down. "Be back in an hour." Lenny rapped his knuckles on the table, left the untouched drink, got up and left. Thinking of the money, knowing he'd be light. Maybe he could take it from the joint savings, but he bet Paulina had already got to it.

Luís giving him another address, saying this place was closing after the game, that they'd meet him there. "And don't forget the piece."

. . . take the money

"What do we think?" Luís said, looking from Jaco to Carlos.

"They got people for this," Carlos said.

"He don't want Ernie Zimm to know," Luís said.

"Maybe wants to see who we are, the guys stepping in, taking over." Carlos turned to see where the bartender was, raising his empty glass.

The bartender held up three fingers, like it was a question.

"How about you?" Carlos looked at Jaco.

"Want to take the gilete to that babaca." Jaco slipped a thumb across his windpipe.

"I mean a drink?" Carlos said, got a no, and held two fingers to the bartender.

"We take his money, then go see this jeweler," Luís said. "After, you can do what you want."

The bartender came and set down fresh drinks, taking Lenny's untouched glass.

. . . *no perry mason*

S tretching out a hand, the guy said, "Gabe, I'm Ross Cohen."
This curly-headed putz was supposed to get him off.
To Gabe, he looked fresh out of law school. The briefcase
looked like it just came off a rack at Grand & Toy, not a
scuff on it. What the hell was Ernie Zimm doing sending
in a rookie?

"You know how long I been waiting?" Gabe Zoller looked
him over, slow to shake the hand. He was in the deep shit,
looking at second-degree murder on two counts, and Ernie
sends him a lawyer with soft hands. And nearly a day later,
leaving him to stew in the piss stench of holding.

"I'm your lawyer, Gabe, not your cabbie. And so we're
clear, you're not the only guy who got himself jammed up,
swearing on his sainted mother he's wrongly accused."

"Just get me the fuck out of here."

"And I'm no magician."

"Tell me I'm not your first case." Gabe looked doubtful.

"I'm the guy that goes to the wall for you, doing what I
can. But if you want to shop around, be my guest. I'll take
that back to Ernie, let him know how you feel. No? Then

lose the attitude and let's get to it. I got someplace to be."
Ross Cohen looked at his watch like he was running late.

"This thing's a frame-up." Gabe leaned back in the wooden chair, the cuffs limiting his motion. "You got a smoke?"

Ross Cohen frowned and shook his head.

"Look, I was shopping on Spadina, checking in a window, when the blues come with the red lights flashing, throwing me to the ground. My chicken hits the pavement."

"You hand me drek, that's what I get to work with, drek. You want to guess the chances of a reduced sentence?"

"The hell do you want?"

"I want to know what happened. Let me take it from there."

Gabe looked at him, then at the gray walls, saying, "Maybe they got this box bugged."

"I only wish." Ross Cohen glanced up, saying, "Then I go find a judge, tell him the law's interfering with attorney-client privilege, you kidding? Have the jury believing they framed you, tampered with evidence, coerced witnesses. Have a cloud of reasonable doubt floating in the courtroom, and get the whole mess thrown out in a second. Be a beautiful thing."

Gabe narrowed his eyes like he was starting to see it, yeah, maybe this was his guy.

"So, Gabe, have another go, but tell me straight."

Gabe nodded. "The cops got it in for me. That part's true."

Ross Cohen leaned back, looking at him and tapping his pen on the table.

"Maybe I roughed up the chicken guy in the Market, a bit of a misunderstanding, then helped myself to a bird. They got me there. What's that, grand theft chicken? Drove near this mink guy's place, stopped to get something to go with my supper; pickles, cabbage, or the like."

"Brought the chicken with you?"

"Woulda cooked in the car, so I took it with, yeah. Minding my own when they jumped me, saying I did it. And why the fuck would a man shove a gun up a chicken?"

Ross Cohen set the pen down, pinched his lower lip, saying, "Two eyewitnesses, plus they have the murder weapon, one they're sure they'll find your prints on."

"All part of their frame-up."

"We're going to need more than reasonable doubt here, Gabe. I go in with your story, I'm going to get blindsided by the truth — a lot of that in this case. You not see that?"

Gabe nodded, thinking he had to let this guy spin it the way they taught him in Osgoode. "You want me confessing to a murder rap?"

"I need to see what's coming, Gabe. Trying to make that clear to you."

"So let's say I did it."

"Then first thing, we put some distance between you and Ernie, the man running a legit travel business."

"You saving me or him?"

"You're the one on the ledge, Gabe. I'm trying to soften the landing."

Gabe tried to fold his arms but couldn't due to the cuffs.

Sighing, Ross opened his case, pulled out papers, saying, "Come on, Gabe, I shouldn't have to explain how this works. First thing the Crown attorney does, he drags in your past." Ross reading from a sheet, "Assault with a weapon, aggravated assault, sexual assault, sexual with a weapon. A couple of them sticking."

"Meaning what?"

"Meaning, I'm your lawyer, not your rabbi. I don't judge what you did. You tell me straight, and let me do the rest. That way, I don't walk into court and get ambushed by the facts."

"Okay, let's say I did it."

"Yeah, let's say that."

"But no way I'm pleading to it."

"I'm in the business of doubt, Gabe. I create enough of it, and the case gets pitched. That's how the game's played."

"So you saying I plead not guilty?"

"The only guilty there is."

Gabe nodded, then said, "With Ernie taking care of the witnesses ..."

Cohen raised a hand. "I don't know about that, but I guess it happens."

"Okay, maybe I was in that neck of the woods, passing by this Merchant of whatever, looking for a grocery joint. The hell would I want with a fur in June anyway, right? Haven't even got a girl to give it to. There's the landlady, sure, but it's not that kind of thing."

Cohen tapped his pen on the table.

"So the cops must've spotted me, on account of my priors — like you said — answering the gunshot call, grabbed me up on account of my priors. Me, I just spit on a sidewalk and they jump from the bushes. Got to be what happened?" Gabe liked the sound of it, asking about bail.

"Told you I don't do magic."

"So, what, I'm stuck in this pissy hell?"

"Any judge'll see you heading for Buffalo as soon as you're out the door. But I'll talk with the Crown's man, see about pushing up the date, try to get you held someplace with a better smell." Ross Cohen knowing all about the Don, the old city jail where this guy'd likely end up. Then looked at his watch, saying, "That's it for now. You know to keep it zipped, right?"

"I'm not that dumb."

Ross rose from his chair, checking his watch again, saying, "Could be tomorrow before I can see the Crown. Just sit tight, and I'll get back soon as I can. Anything you want me to pass on to Mr. Zimm?"

"What I got to say, I say myself."

"Understand, the man's got to insulate himself." Ross Cohen went to the door, then turned. "Oh, a name he asked me to pass on . . ."

Gabe looked at him.

"Poppy."

The name didn't mean anything to him, Gabe watching him reach in a pocket of his case, setting down a Polaroid, turning it the right way around for Gabe to see, saying, "Meet Poppy."

A pock-face girl of maybe twenty-one, a ruffled crop-top showing her belly above unzipped cut-off jeans, her hand like it was sliding inside. Her eyes looked glazed, her mouth a mess of lipstick, twisted into a smile.

Cohen said, "Dances at the Zanzibar. Believe you frequent the place."

"Yeah, Poppy, sure — go-go gal all hips and arms, jumping around. Can't believe what she does on that pole. A couple bucks and she does it in private, sits in your lap, man . . ."

"Good times, I bet. More important, you were with her the time of the shooting. Maybe you two got to talking after her work, gave her a lift, took Spadina on your way home and dropped her off. Maybe you're starting to remember now?"

"Poppy doing my pole, the cubicle of the men's room."

"Why there?"

"The type of thing a jury'll buy, no?"

Cohen sighed.

"But understand, I never paid for it in my life."

"An upstanding citizen like yourself." Cohen reached for the photo.

Gabe leaned back, looking at it, thinking about it, saying, "Poppy, yeah, the girl went crazy for me. Worked up an appetite, maybe stopped off for a chicken, figured I wanted to watch her cook it up. I get out of here, sure like to go pay my respects, give her my thanks."

"Yeah, bet she'd like that." Tucking the photo away, Ross Cohen closed his case, looked like he might be sick, and he got up.

"So, bail. You gonna try, right?"

"I'll be in touch." With that, Ross Cohen went and rapped on the door.

"And bring me smokes next time. Mark Tens."

Then the door opened and Ross Cohen was gone.

... *money with menace*

"Call me that again, and Jaco gives you a zipper." Luís drew a finger across his windpipe, same way Jaco had done. Tucking Lenny's money in a pocket, six hundred more, Lenny having to promise the rest.

"Portu-guys?" Acting surprised, Lenny grinned at this guy with his Sonny Bono hair, then at the two brothers with mustaches that looked like a kid drew them on with a crayon. Watching his money disappear, saying, "Just figured if one's Portuguese, then more ought to be ... forget it."

Standing near the door, he looked at the three of them in back of this place called the Rio Tinto, another dark joint smelling of fried fish and stale drink, with a painted rooster over the bar, these guys watching their Seleção das Quinas, a replay of the same World Cup qualification match on CBC. Couldn't call it soccer around these guys, likely get his throat cut for disrespect. In their world it was futebol — and it was life and death. Their team wanting to make the cut for next year's Cup — the first time in history they made it. These guys making the sign of the cross. Eyes to Heaven, Luís put his hands together, muttering a prayer to the rooster for the Seleção to hoist the Cup. And God help anybody saying anything different. Didn't matter their team could face the champs out of Brazil, hosted by the English, and all the powerhouses of Europe, all chomping at the bit. These guys believing they had the deus do futebol on their side.

Luís glanced from the TV, saying, "We'll talk . . ."

Lenny looking at them, their eyes glued to the set after their team scored an early goal, fourteen minutes in.

"You know I'm good for the rest."

"You don't like how we do it, what's that word?" Luís flicked his fingers, eyes on the match.

"Panache," Jaco said without turning.

"Yeah, panache," Luís said.

"Okay, give me back the cash." Lenny looked to the door, saying, "I'll go see the Jamaicans, let you catch your game."

Luís snapped his fingers, pointed to an empty chair.

Lenny stood looking at their backs, guessed they were waiting on a commercial before talking business. A spot finally coming on about Pond's Skin Cream.

Luís turned to him. "This jewelry store, what's so special?"

"Like I said, there's this woman . . ."

"What woman?"

"One that works there."

"Another show? You come in, hit me with a pistol and rescue the place, maybe get the woman?"

The brothers grinned.

"This one's no show."

Luís considered. "A thing like that's gonna cost . . ."

"Already agreed on that. Plus you help yourself to anything in the place."

"What the cops call evidence."

"That's up to you."

"Jewelers carry. Deli guys don't," Luís said. "For this, the wet work ..." Luís sounding like he was ringing up a sale. "Gotta be a grand each."

These guys still trying to shake him down. Lenny watching a TV spot about Johnson's Wax.

Then the game was back on, Portugal moving the ball through midfield.

"Two Gs, counting what's in your pocket."

Luís shook his head, saying, "That's for hearing you out."

"Twenty-five hundred and take what you want." Looking at the back of their heads, Lenny thinking of drawing the .32 and winging one of the brothers, show he wasn't playing. Or shoot all three, take his money back and go talk to the Jamaicans. Still, he could picture Paulina looking up from behind the counter, seeing Luís walk in, pull a piece and let her see it coming. And there would be no lawyers. And no Get. Lenny would be out twenty-five hundred, plus the cost of the funeral and the flowers. He'd stand graveside while the rabbi spoke his words and the women wailed. Then toss a handful of dirt and sit through the condolence meal. Then he'd go back to his house, get that armchair down from the rafters and get on with his life.

"Gonna ask again, who's the woman?" Luís said over a shoulder.

"Okay, my ex."

Luís nodded like he understood, saying, "We'll let you know." Then waved him off.

"You already took my money."

Luís nodded, yeah he did.

All three coming out of their chairs as Portugal moved the ball now, a strong drive up the infield. The team hungry with the single-goal lead. Leaning toward the tube, all of them growling with their hands in fists. Portugal giving up the ball, the momentum going the other way. Offense and midfield running back, defending against a Romanian threat. Countering, catching a break and driving the ball back up the field, the offense running like rabbits — Lenny thinking what a dumb game. The three of these guys groaning, then jumping out of their chairs, arms up, as Eusébio, the one called the Black Panther, caught a break and ran like a son of a bitch, splitting the defenders and kicking the ball past the diving goalie, his second goal of the match. Arms in the air, eyes popping out of the man's head, mouth open in a yell. Dropping to his knees in the end zone, hands in prayer, the team rushing up and diving on him. The entire crowd in Lisbon going crazy, Luís and the brothers jumping like fire ants were gorging in their shorts, everybody in the Rio Tinto yelling "*Goooool*" and hugging each other. Hands together, tears, prayers going to the rooster.

And Lenny ducked out of there.

. . . timekeepers of the world

A stack of payables to the left, receivables to the right. Paulina's mind drifted from the entries and updating the books. What had she been thinking, marrying a guy like Lenny? Bad enough she got in bed with him way back when, not sure what she'd been thinking. Living with his lies and neglect for two long years. She came back to work after the lunch with Gary Evans, writing checks and licking envelopes and stamps, sitting at the desk in the rear. Feeling guilty about it.

Watching her poppa up front behind the glass case, dealing with his customers. Thoughts going from Lenny to Gary, then back to the weight of Lenny. Paulina looking at it from all sides. She was right asking for the Get. And Gary was a good-looking guy, not from the tribe, but for a goy he was one of the good ones. Knowing Gary had more than lunch on his mind, the way he'd been looking at her over dessert. Paulina tasting the chocolate, pushing away thoughts of the two of them in bed. Then smiling to herself, hoping he could do it without clicking his teeth.

She'd slow things down, tell Gary she needed to be sure.

Tell him she had to be done with Lenny first. Wondering how her poppa would take the news.

Seeing him talking to a handsome couple, heading for their first anniversary, showing them a black onyx daisy necklace on a gold chain, a design by Mary Quant, the one who designed the miniskirt. Mentioned the lay-away plan, letting them decide. Paulina betting the young hubby had been hooked at "miniskirt." But, her poppa wasn't a hard-sell — had a way of making folks feel easy, a man you could trust. Amazing how he remembered customers by name, even years later.

And the referrals and repeat business just kept coming like the tide. A kind and gentle man in spite of the dark years he'd lived through. She wondered if he ever thought about those awful times when he lay alone in his bed at night — if he had nightmares about it.

Trusting, but careful too, Poppa having the mantrap installed, two ugly doors with the switches behind his glass counter. Red for the outer door, black for the inner. Isaac Levine explaining to anyone who asked, the mantrap kept his honest customers safe, and the lower insurance helped keep the prices down. Paulina had to smile, Poppa sounding like his friend Edwin Mirvish, except unlike Ed, he didn't go around telling everyone he was honest.

Watching him ring it up, selling the young couple the necklace, along with the matching stud-earrings at cost, Isaac pressing the black button, then the red, wishing them a good day and letting them out. Paulina back to thinking about Gary when the elderly gent came in and picked up an inscribed Cartier, a retirement present for years of service. Doing a few entries, she tried to recall the last time she had good sex, then thinking it was too warm in the shop, stepping over to the thermostat, adjusting the dial.

Isaac showed a doctor the Rolex display, calling the line the timekeepers of the world, explaining how each timepiece was made in-house, about its perpetual movement and the hundreds of finely crafted components carefully assembled by hand, the doctor going off to decide between the Day-Date in eighteen-carat and the Explorer with the Oyster bracelet. Isaac appraising an estate necklace and ring set for a wealthy customer, taking it in on consignment. Then, when the shop was empty again, he looked at her, asked if she was alright, told her she looked flushed.

"Just a bit of a headache."

"Could go for some of Mica's matzo ball soup. How about you?" Isaac wondering aloud where the day went and patting his stomach.

"Not so hungry." Paulina blaming it on licking stamps, didn't mention the lunch with Gary, but offering to get him something.

"It's a slow day, you should go home." Looked at her like he saw past her migraines and her troubles with Lenny, the marital split hanging like a black cloud. He didn't need to say it, she knew he'd agree she was right to leave him.

"I have plenty to do, Poppa."

"There's always time for plenty tomorrow."

"How about first I get your matzo?"

"I'll call Mica to send the kid. So it costs me a tip. Go on, *shoo*." He swept with his hands.

She frowned, but thinking she could use a rest, to lie in her bed and let the migraine pass. Getting up from the desk, she reached her purse and kissed the top of his head, saying, "You're right, Poppa." Wondering if she'd gotten taller or if he was getting shorter.

"Of course I'm right." Isaac picked up the phone, dialing Mica's.

. . . man trapped

The dark-haired man outside the security door looked at the window display and into the shop, then at the speaker in the thick glass, the kind they had at movie theaters. Careful not to glance up at the surveillance camera above his shoulder.

Isaac Levine watched him on the monitor — a square bandage above the man's right temple, bruised skin showing past the hairline. Not a customer he recognized. Then looking at the car he got out of, a midsize Pontiac in the lot behind him, dark green, with two guys sitting in front, both with mustaches, both looking this way. The driver kept the engine running. Isaac seeing it for what it was, thinking he should call the cops, but so far, where was the crime? And on top, he was curious to see how they planned to do it.

"How may I help you?" he spoke into the intercom.

"Well, I've got this watch and could be I'm interested in selling it. Heard you're the guy to see."

"Could you hold it to the camera?"

The guy looked up, like he was surprised there was a camera, then held up his wrist, showing the watch, careful to turn his face.

Isaac looked at it, saying, "A Submariner."

"It says Rolex on it," the guy said, holding it closer.

"A Rolex Submariner, a diver's watch."

"Diver, that right?"

"Can go down a hundred meters."

"Why'd anybody do that?" The guy smiled, glancing to the parking lot.

"For that, you have to ask a diver," Isaac said.

"Got left to me by an uncle."

"Guess he was the diver then."

"Didn't know him so well. Man lived in the old country, maybe he did his diving there. Thing is, I want to find out what it's worth, seeing I don't even swim."

"So there's no sentiment?" Isaac said.

"No, clean as a whistle." Holding it to the lens again.

Isaac nodded and buzzed open the inner door.

"Like *Candid Camera* in here, huh?" The man smiled, coming to the counter, looking around the store, one more glance back to the running Pontiac, the two men still inside.

"Just had the system put in."

"Makes it like Fort Knox, all secure, huh?"

"You feel safe, right?"

"Sure I do."

Isaac let the guy who didn't dive slip it off, holding the Rolex in his hand. Saying, "Oh, and my buddy was hoping to get a look around, the one at the wheel's getting married." Pointing out to the parking lot. "Time to get her a ring, you know, make it official. You got somebody else working can help him out?" The guy looking around for anybody else in the shop.

"Think I can take care of you both." Isaac smiled, thinking a couple of moves ahead. After he had ordered the matzo from Mica's he heard about the robbery attempt from his nephew: three guys, two of them with mustaches. Then Lenny happened to walk in, saving the day.

The man turned and wagged his finger to the car.

The passenger got out and walked easy to the door.

"Thought the driver's getting married?"

"Yeah, them two, almost like twins, always get them mixed up."

Isaac buzzed the man in, one door, then the other, both men inside now. The third one still in the car with the engine running, gray exhaust coming from the pipe. He was watching this way. Isaac smiled and said to the man with the mustache, "So, I hear congratulations are in order."

"Yeah, tying the knot." The man didn't look happy about it, saying, "A good girl and not uh ..." Making a sign of pregnant with his hands.

"Sounds like she deserves a fine setting then." Isaac pointed to the display of engagement rings to his far right, saying he had something for everybody, and something in every price range. Then he looked back to the one with the Rolex, setting a velvet cloth on the glass top, inviting him to set the watch down.

The man did, saying, "You use one of them loupes?"

"I use the eyes of a hawk." Isaac smiled, picking up the watch, keeping both men in sight, then saying, "This one's a '57, a tiny scratch here on the crystal." Pointing to it. "But a fine piece. Cost a hundred and fifty when it was new." Isaac checked the back, then the bracelet, then looked at the man.

"So, what d'you think?"

"Think you'll be happy knowing it's gone up in value."

"That so, worth a lot, huh?"

"Well, I can give you two-twenty, be more except for the scratch. Just need to check the registration. You happen to have the papers?" Isaac knowing he didn't.

"Sure, got it right here." The man reached for his pocket.

The other man looked out the window and nodded, then stepped closer.

The first man's hand was coming from the pocket as Isaac vaulted the counter, like he was light as air. Landing between the two men, clutching the first man's wrist with his left hand, catching him by surprise. A sharp jerk downward, then back up, and he twisted the wrist, snapping the pistol free with his right hand, striking the butt against the bandage on his temple — a dull thump.

Turning, Isaac shoved the pistol in the second man's face, a razor raised in a hand. The first man slumped to his knees, flopping against the glass case, then went face-first to the floor.

"Tua loucura you fuck, the man's trying to sell you a watch." Mustache man froze, then backed a step, the straight razor out to the side, looking at his unconscious friend.

Keeping the pistol on him, Isaac went back behind his counter, sounding calm, saying, "You want to shave while I call it in? Go right ahead."

"How about we clear out? You never see us again." The man closed the razor, seeing the uselessness of it, putting it away.

The third man was out of the car, standing by his door like he wasn't sure what to do.

Isaac set the pistol on the glass, reached under and pressed the red button, the inner door opening, waving a hand, saying, "Shoo."

The man looked to his buddy on the floor, then out to the one by the car. Lifting up the unconscious man, he got him through the door. Isaac pressing the button and the inner door closed, and the man was left holding his buddy in the tight space, realizing they were caught between the doors, pounding at the glass with his free hand, propping up his unconscious buddy.

The third man stood helpless, looking at the trapped men.

Letting that guy figure it out, Isaac picked up the receiver and dialed the police, spoke calmly, saying there was a robbery attempt at Isaac's Jewelers, giving the address, the trapped man yelling and punching at the bulletproof glass.

Leaning his buddy against the inner door, the mustache-man took the razor to the glass, slashing like he was Zorro, trying to cut his way out. The third man stood in the lot, still not sure what to do, finally getting back behind the wheel and peeling out of there.

Grinning, Isaac told the dispatcher, "Tell the boys not to rush. Oh, before I forget, the plate on the getaway car ..." Isaac said the four digits and the letter C into the phone, then said, "And maybe send an ambulance, looks like one banged his head." Hanging up, he set the man's Colt on the velvet, picked up the Rolex and looked at it, then set it in the top drawer and shut it. Then he waited, the mustache man still yelling, pounding and slashing at the mantrap door, the other one out on the floor, the third one long gone. Isaac looked at the monitor, then studied the knobs, wondering which one was the record button.

. . . *face to the music*

G ary Evans pushed past the twin doors, going into the 52nd, nodded to a couple of uniforms going out, heard O'Riordan, the bloated desk sergeant on the phone. He held out a note, put a hand over the mouthpiece, told Gary, "Some detective called for you."

"What detective?" Gary said, the name Isaac Levine scrawled on the paper, then an address with a couple of the numbers scratched out, then the name Lenny Ovitz.

"I look like your secretary?" The sergeant got it under control, muttered the phone had been ringing all day, then, "Think he said he was from the 32nd, something about a robbery attempt at a jeweler's up on Lawrence, the name I wrote." Tapping at the note. "Said maybe it ties to a case you're working. Wanted to give you the heads up. That's it, all he said." The sarge going back to his call.

Waiting for the sarge to hang up, Gary said. "That's it, you call that a message?"

O'Riordan made a face and shrugged, muttering something like he wasn't some girl Friday.

Taking his badge off his belt, Gary held it up. "See there, says we're on the same team. You want I can call the lieut, let him explain it to you."

Those sorry red eyes on him, O'Riordan repeated what he remembered about the call, then said, "Like I said, it's been hell of a day."

Clipping the badge on his belt, Gary said thanks, then went to his desk in back, checked the address and went back out the front door, giving the sarge a wave.

Paulina's maiden name was Levine, before she married the dirtbag Ovitz. Like any cop, Gary wasn't big on coincidence, getting in the Plymouth and driving to the address. The two perps already taken to holding by the time he pulled into the lot.

Walking under Isaac the Jeweler's sign, knowing what it would mean — Paulina thinking he taught science to teenagers, Gary signing their names for court time at her club. Stamping out the butt of his smoke, he rapped on the outer door, ready with his questions.

She was going to find out sooner or later. Didn't want to admit it, but he had been hoping he'd end up in her bed before she found out. Playing singles and taking it one lie at a time — Gary going from tennis to thinking about her that way.

Holding his shield up to the glass, waiting for the uniform inside to figure out how to work the mantrap doors and buzz him in.

"You're new, huh?" Gary said to this kid a few years past high school, standing in his blues. Going to the counter and stretching out his hand, meeting Isaac Levine. Seeing the resemblance — the father calm and smiling, the eyes that looked at you and knew who you were. And for his size this old man had the kind of grip that got your attention. Gary putting away his shield, telling Isaac he had a few questions, thinking this botched robbery could be connected to an ongoing investigation, all part of the same swamp.

Letting the jacket fall over the shield, he wanted to know the step by step, how it happened, saying, "Take your time, Mr. Levine. Just tell it in your own words."

"Who else's words would I use?" Isaac smiled, told him to call him by his first name, and he laid it out, how he saw the car pull up, one guy getting out, coming in to sell a watch, a second man coming in, another one behind the wheel.

"Three guys to sell one watch," Gary said. "So you saw it coming."

"Couldn't miss it."

"But you opened the door." Could be this old boy had squirrels in the attic, but Gary was liking him, looking at the mantrap doors.

"Wanted to see how it worked," Isaac said, explaining about the entry system. "Just had it put in last week. Making sure I got my money's worth, you understand?"

"You been robbed before, Isaac?"

"Not even close."

Gary smiled, picturing him jumping the counter and snapping the pistol from a guy half his age, then knocking him out with it. Putting it on his accomplice, trapping them both and holding them for police. Even got the plate of the getaway car, and gave a fair description of the driver. A pretty sharp squirrel. Most folks this guy's age walked with a cane and dropped their teeth in a glass, giving up gin for Geritol. Then Gary was back to wondering how Paulina was going to take the news, finding out he didn't know a beaker from a flask.

"If God lived down here, crazies like that would break his windows. Bet you bump into your share, detective."

"I could tell you stories, Isaac. And call me Gary."

"When guys like that come, you get to show who you are — can make you feel alive. Right now, I just shaved off ten years."

"Yeah, I get that." Gary nodded, thinking how his old man had worked at Stelco for forty years, never took a chance in his life, struggled just to get out of his armchair and emptied his bladder every hour. Could set one of Isaac Levine's watches to it.

"Just sorry I didn't get all three," Isaac said.

"Let me earn my pay, okay?" Asking Isaac to show him the wrist lock, how he unarmed the guy.

"Just used his own force against him," Isaac said, demonstrating the move by taking Gary's forearm, getting him to stand the way the robber had stood, turning his wrist, twisted his hips and nearly put Gary on the floor. Giving him a wink. "Nothing to it."

"Any combat training, something like that?"

"Maybe I watch too much *Peter Gunn*. You know it, the show?"

"Yeah, sure, it's a good one, and I love the music. Hard to get it out of my head."

"That Mancini, yeah, he's something."

"Isaac, you keep a gun in the place?" Gary knowing jewelers were allowed carry permits.

"I got my doors, it's enough." He smiled, saying, "My Paulina, she carries. Makes her feel safe. You should meet her, ask her some questions." His eyes danced.

"Paulina, huh?" Gary feeling the twist down in the pit.

"My daughter works here. Today, I sent her home early."

"And she missed seeing her old man in action."

"Not so old, please."

"Yeah, I guess you proved that." Gary thinking he ought to act professional, bringing them back on course, saying, "So, you saw it coming, but you let it happen, opening the door . . ."

"Punks needed a lesson."

"You could've been shot."

"The day I get shot by punks, then it's my time." Isaac waved a hand.

Gary smiled, saying, "One more question, Isaac. And understand, it's one I have to ask. You on any kind of medication?"

The old man laughed and shook his head. "Not even Alka-Seltzer." Looking out the window to where the getaway car had parked, the smile growing.

Turning in the same direction, Gary was looking to the parking lot, his own smile fading. Paulina put a leg out of her Wagonaire, stepping out and coming toward the door, looking worried, speaking to the uniform out front, Gary seeing the worry turn to surprise, the tennis-playing science teacher at the glass display talking to her poppa, taking notes. Gary's shield hanging from his belt. Not knowing what else to do, he gave a half-hearted wave, felt like he was sinking.

. . . father time staring down

"**Y**ou say death penalty and expect me to shit my pants." Gabe Zoller looked at the Crown attorney. He had overheard two of the bulls talking about it, how Gabe had it coming, both willing to pay to see it, the trap dropping and the rope snapping his spine, a befitting end for a scum-plug like Zoller — dying and soiling himself. One guard saying the needle was too good and quick, the rope befitting the rap.

"And a good show." The other bull laughed, saying, "Be something, seeing the hangman slide the greased plank under his feet, watch him drop, hear that dry snap, the shit running down his kicking legs."

The other one said, "If the drop doesn't do it, there's the gurgle. Yeah, wouldn't mind watching his feet fox trotting in air while shitting himself."

The two of them laughing, telling Gabe about the one convict who'd been hanged at the old Don before their time; a badly tied knot had the soused hangman doing the deed twice. Another time the same hangman was on a full-on stink-o drunk and didn't get the knot right, and he had to jump on and grab the condemned man around the legs, adding his own weight to help the man cross to his reward. Quite the show for the guards and the warden.

Gabe told Terrence Dow he wouldn't mind looking up those jailers on the outside. See if they'd be laughing then.

"I'm not seeking it," Terrence Dow said. "Not at this time." Dow knowing like everybody else in the justice system, since Pearson's Liberals took power, capital punishment cases were being commuted. Gabe Zoller was looking at twenty-five years for the double murders, with no likelihood of parole for fifty. Meaning he'd live on prison chow, spending his days behind bars, and with nobody in his life, he'd end in an unloved grave. Unless Ernie Zimm's people got to him, the D.O.s finding him iced, lying shanked or with his skull caved in. Any way it happened, this town would see itself better off.

"Guess you think that's a comfort." Gabe looked at him like he wouldn't mind meeting him on the outside along with the two bulls.

"You play it right, Gabe, and maybe I can get you transferred."

"We playing footsie now? Tell me, your game come with bail?"

"Now we're talking fairy tales."

"How about you spell it out then."

Stepping to the door, Terrence Dow tapped on it, getting the guard to open up. Saying to Gabe, "Let's say it's a give and take."

"Yeah, well I'm no rat."

"I'm not judging you," Dow said.

"You think Ernie Zimm'll sit on his hands if he finds out we're talking right now?"

"Like I said, I can get you transferred out."

"Man's got ties in and out, and all over. Means he'll find me and get to me anytime he wants."

"One thing you've got in your favor . . ."

"What's that?"

"You're no use to me dead."

"I just told you, the man's got people all over." Gabe lowered his voice, glancing to the tiny barred window. "Some on duty."

Terrence Dow looked at him, knowing the truth of it, but saying, "Exactly why it's important we work something out — something that works both ways."

"How about start with this." Gabe lifted his cuffed wrist — the links rattling against the table leg — wanting them taken off.

"Everything you give me gets you something, like a point system."

"Except I got to trust you up front."

"Give me enough and you'll be doing time with the stockbrokers at Beaver Creek — better food and guards in a good humor, and no Ernie Zimm. Guarantee you that."

"How about no jail time?"

Terrence Dow smiled.

Gabe eyed him, this ambulance-chaser playing with him.

"I get you transferred out, then I need something to take upstairs, something that shows the love, you understand?"

Gabe tried folding his arms again, the cuffs not letting him do it. "I'll talk to my shyster. See what he says."

Dow gathered his papers, dropping them in his case.

"I got names, enough to make you drool. You want them, I need more'n some medium joint and better chow. How about some parole, a chunk of time shaved off?"

"Give me some meat, show me you're being straight, and I'll talk to the higher-ups."

137

"Everything's right here." Tapping his temple. "Keep you busy all your lawyer days. Like I said, enough to make you drool."

"Show me yours and I show you mine. How it works. And not the something that every kid on the Market corners already knows."

"Ernie gets wind, and you know how this ends."

"Going to take faith on both sides."

Gabe looked at him, felt his feet on that trap door, shaking his head like he had nothing to say.

"I get how you feel, Gabe. And I think, deep down, you know I'm your best shot. You suppose even if Ernie Zimm tampers and gets you out of this, think he's going to forgive this one? Think again. Tell you what, you sit with it a while. You want to talk, bang on the door, the guard'll get me word. Only I wouldn't take too long."

. . . feet on a trap door

Terrence Dow had pushed it, but he got Zoller's attention — dumb as he was, the man had to know Ernie Zimm wasn't going to sit back and see how it turned out. Maybe Zimm could tamper with the case, and maybe not. Without a deal, Zoller was staring at life with consecutive stretches of parole ineligibility. Meaning he'd be inside for the next half century. Handing over Zimm had a better outlook, meaning he'd be locked up in a better place, with the kind of parole that left a light down a long tunnel. Dow realizing if the boss even thought Zoller was thinking about it, he'd be shanked before he got to the Jell-O at the mainline chow. He snapped the clasps of his case shut and got set to leave.

"You don't know these people," Gabe said.

"But I plan to."

"No place he can't reach."

"Like I said, I'll put you in a safe house until the trial, with a guard by the door, day and night. And an upgrade on the slop the Don calls chow."

"Yeah, where's this place?"

"You know how to find out." Terrence looked at him, this man ready to plunge — the fear behind his eyes. Going off the script now, saying, "You know, Gabe, it gets me, guys like you . . ."

"Guys like me?"

"The killer playing the victim, acting like I ought to have a soft spot."

"Yeah, maybe I look you up when I get out."

"How old you going to be then? What, run me over in your wheelchair?" Terrence Dow got up, knowing he might be throwing it away. Going to the door and banging the corner of his briefcase against it.

The guard looked through the glass, turned the lock and stood aside and let the Crown attorney through.

Gabe said, "This place you're talking about, it got a TV?"

Dow turned at the door, saying, "Better than that, I'll get your trial moved up. You want that, then I need more than the scraps you want to toss."

Gabe leaned back. "And a carton of smokes, Mark Tens, filter tips."

"First, I need a name."

Gabe sucked at his teeth, waited and finally sighed, then said, "Lenny Ovitz."

. . . a space between the lies

"Well, I can't wait to hear it." Paulina was looking at him, then pinching Gary's sleeve, tugging him aside, out of Isaac's earshot. And stood facing him.

Gary thought he was ready for this, but he was having trouble finding the words.

"So, you teach kids chemistry and biology, play a little tennis. And on the side, a little Agatha Christie?" She folded her arms, saying, "You're just full of surprises, Gary. Is that even your name, Gary?"

"I should've been straight up."

"You think so?" Smiling at him.

"Look, Paulina, it started as an undercover thing, looking into racketeering." Keeping his voice low. "And your husband's name came up . . ."

"You mean my ex."

"Okay, ex. And one thing led to another." Gary hearing his own words, how ridiculous he sounded.

"So I'm the ex of a guy you want to arrest. Just a gold-mine of facts and figures." A hand going to her hip.

"I'm sorry, Paulina. Maybe it started out like that ..." Gary gave up, couldn't make it sound right.

"I'm sorry I let you win."

And he looked at her.

"Oh, come on. I could've handed you your butt every set, anytime I wanted. And so you know, your forehand needs work. But the male ego being the egg it is, I couldn't let the big boy feel like he got spanked. So I held back, went for the net instead of the easy ace, volleyed balls out, serving double faults. So, guess I wasn't straight either."

He looked at her, deciding if she was kidding.

"So, is it?"

"What?"

"Your real name."

"Middle one's Bernard."

"The name of a big, dumb dog. That supposed to make up for it, giving me Bernard?" Looking past him at Isaac standing by the Rolex case, her poppa pretending not to be listening. Taking Gary by the sleeve, she edged him toward the engagement rings, saying, "So having lunch was more about nailing Lenny. Nailing me's the booby prize."

"I can't talk about an ongoing investigation."

"Nice for you. And when you're done with your investigating, you ought to get yourself a real Barbie, tall and thin and believing everything you say, the kind that giggles when you talk. Maybe teach her that serve."

"I'm not that guy, the one you think."

"Are we done, Detective Bernard?" She gave him cold eyes a moment more, then turned to Isaac inspecting the back of a watch, saying, "My poppa's ears are burning."

Giving a tight smile, Gary tucked his notepad inside his jacket, went and thanked Isaac for his time and stepped to the door.

Isaac pressed the buttons, red, then black, letting the detective out, hearing him ask the uniform outside the door what he was looking at. Then going to his Plymouth, and Gary Evans drove away. The rookie uniform getting in his cruiser and doing the same.

"He seems nice," Isaac said, studying an Omega from the repair shelf.

"Don't even start, Poppa."

"Seems you two already met." Isaac took his case knife, popping the pressure back-case off, setting the watch on his cloth, examining the works inside.

Paulina looked out the window, drawing a breath like she was sucking the air out of the room, saying, "Why, Poppa?"

"I couldn't help it, but I guess he was going to tell you —"

"I mean you, jumping over the counter."

"I still got it, huh?" He smiled.

"Not common sense, no, not a bit."

"Three men drive up and want to rob me. So . . . I tried out my doors. Showing you the value."

"A child with his new toy."

"Had to see they lived up to promise."

"What's the point of talking to you? You'll never change."

He set the Omega aside, opened the drawer and took Luís's Rolex, reached one of his tags from a cardboard box, wrote $225 on it, tied the loop around the band and set it with the pre-owned watches.

"Why are men like that?"

"Like what?"

"They look in your eyes and lie through their teeth."

"How did I lie?"

"Who's talking about you?" Feeling the bitter down her throat, the burn in back of her eyes, another migraine coming on.

"You lost me, ketsele." Isaac going to her, putting a hand to her shoulder, then taking her in a hug, letting her take her time.

And the crying taps were on, and she leaned into him, and he held her, the way he'd always done, and she sank into him. Poppa protecting her from the world.

"Find something good." He kept his voice easy, talking to his little girl.

She nodded like she understood.

His arms circled around her, held her like one of them was dying, and he rocked her, not sure if this was about Lenny or something else, but knowing she'd come around and tell him.

... *down in the ward*

"Looks like opposing counsel's taking it to the wall."
Ross Cohen said it matter of fact, looking at Ernie
Zimm, stepping into the man's office and closing the door.

"The fuck you saying?" Ernie looked like he might throw
the desk set.

"Think they're cooking a deal."

"You tell him, the go-go girl on the pole?"

"Could be they're reducing his sentence."

"Yeah, and I'm cutting off his pecker. He think of that?"

Ross Cohen straightened, like he remembered who he
was talking to.

"Got people seeing the witnesses, buying a juror, all that.
And you, what are you doing for me?"

Putting up his hands, Ross Cohen looked like what
more could he do, taking this one on top of a full caseload,
just because Ernie Zimm wanted it.

Ernie looked like he was about to come out of the chair.
"Twist's been with me ten years. Longer than you."

Cohen looked at the ceramic shards on the floor, coffee
stains on the wall, the garbage can tipped on its side. "Look,

Ernie, Mr. Zimm, I went to see Crown counsel, this guy Dow. See what we could hash out, get the dates pushed up. I get there, and his secretary stalls me, has me wait. I'm sitting forty minutes when she picks up a call and tells me Dow's gone for the day. Calling it crossed wires and apologizing on his behalf."

"So the guy played you?"

"And I've got a mind to file it with the Law Society."

Ernie turned to the window and went quiet, considering Gabe Zoller fucking up this bad, then turning rat. And what he should do about it. Turning back to the useless lawyer, saying, "So, to set things right, you wanna go to your Law Society, that what I'm hearing?"

"I can't force him to see me." Ross Cohen looked down at his polished shoes. "Not my fault they got this airtight."

"Let me ask you, how about I get Dag to take you out back, put a bag on your head, teach you the meaning of airtight?" Ernie rose up and drove the chair into the wall behind him. Watching Ross Cohen retreat out of there, shutting the door as he went. Going to the window, Ernie looked out like the answer might be out among the dented trash cans in the alley.

. . . the head of the rat

Manni Schiller and Dag Malek sat looking at each other from their sales desks, Ross Cohen hurrying through the outer office, brushing past the rack of travel pamphlets, getting out of there. Ernie handing the young lawyer his ass on a plate.

Both men picking up their phones and making calls, Schiller putting a call to the Irish sarge at the precinct, Malek calling the courthouse, getting the names of the two middle-aged sisters, Maggie and Agatha Cooke. Pointing their fingers at Gabe, claimed he hurried from the Merchant of Mink right after shots were fired. Both sisters wearing corrective lenses, sitting in the Nash Gabe had blocked against the curb.

Manni playing with the notion of sending one of the Junction crew: a late-night knock on the sisters' door, create the right kind of doubt in their minds. Doubt that would turn to mistaken identity before the case got to trial. If that didn't get it done, a weekend in Miami or a new RCA might do the trick, but one way or the other, the Cooke sisters would recant.

Next up, the cops had Zoller's .38 with his prints all over it, ballistics proving it had been fired. Five hundred bucks and the

Irish cop would have it vanish from the evidence locker. Then, after jury selection, one of the twelve would have a change of heart, likely meaning another RCA would get delivered after hours. The rest would be up to Cohen the fleeing lawyer, introduce the seeds of evidence tampering, create misgivings in the rest of the jurors' minds. And it might take a visit to the chicken-seller down in the Market, get him to rethink the assault charge against Zoller, boil it down to a misunderstanding. Meaning the chicken man and his family would be sitting around another new set too, the Flintstones and the hillbillies playing in living color.

"The fucker's working a deal." Ernie was yelling from his office.

The look passed between Manni and Dag, Dag taking a coin from his pocket and tossing it, clapping it on his wrist, letting Manni call it.

Manni looked at the heads side of the coin, rolled his eyes, getting up and going to the door, waiting.

"I think he's gone rat," Ernie told him.

"Gabe?"

"Who the fuck we talking about? He's gone rat, taking a deal." Ernie leaned back from the desk, giving Manni that shoot-the-messenger look. "Time reduced for naming names, what do you think? My name. Your name. Blame his mama." Ernie's nostrils going in and out like a bull's. Stamping his fist down, saying, "Both of you in here now."

Manni moved aside as Dag stepped in, both taking chairs across from Ernie's desk. Both knowing what was coming next.

. . . *treading the boards*

"**Y**ou okay, Isaac?" Lenny playing the good son-in-law, coming through the inner door, looking concerned, saying, "Just got word from Mica. Said you been robbed."

"Was no robbery." Isaac fanned a hand through the air, unconcerned. "A couple of boys came in, tried to sell me a watch."

"Said they had a gun?" Lenny with creases across his forehead.

"Trying to drive a hard bargain." The old man smiled.

Lenny realizing he had fueled another story, adding to the legend of Isaac Levine. This seventy-two-year-old Johnny Weissmuller, vaulting the counter and snapping the pistol from Luís's hand and knocking the useless fuck out. Now the old man was joking about it, like it was nothing. Jaco, the tough guy with the razor, grabs his buddy and the two try to limp out, and end up pinned between the mantrap doors. Carlos roaring off. This unarmed geriatric going about one-thirty, one-forty tops, taking out the rival gang.

Luís was supposed to go in solo. Should have walked away when he saw the old man was on his own, and no

Paulina in the place. Instead the two of them go in like a pair of Lee Marvins, with Carlos in plain view in the getaway car. What would it take the cops to tie the two robbery attempts together — with all roads leading to Lenny?

Fuck!

He should have gone to the Caribbeans, these Portuguese were all talk and not up to it, their minds on their fucking soccer, calling it futebol. No way they were edging into Ernie Zimm's territory, and no way they were getting the rest of the money he promised.

Isaac looked amused, his eyes doing their dance, saying, "Guess we're both heroes this day."

"You heard about that, uh?"

"Three boys, Mica said. What are the chances?"

"Yeah, guess I didn't think either. Just saw family on the line and I acted, same as you." Lenny shrugged.

"Think maybe the same three?" Isaac kept smiling.

"It was two. Mica said two came in."

"Two came in, with one in the car. That one not waiting around when I trapped his pals."

"First Mica, now you? I mean, what's going on in this town?"

"You tell me?"

Lenny shrugged. Fuck, he hated this old man.

"One thing for sure, I still got it," Isaac said.

"You really jumped the counter, huh?"

"Could see it in the man's eyes, he didn't have it." Isaac kept looking at Lenny. "Surprised what you see in a man's eyes."

"And the guy being armed." Lenny pretending to look impressed.

"But not for long."

"Took him by surprise — all that training back in the day. Gymnastics, right?"

"Lenny, once you get on the pommel horse, you never get off."

"Well, I'm just glad you're okay, Poppa." Lenny looked around the place like he was making sure it was secure. "So, what can I do?"

"Lenny, just showing up is plenty." Isaac kept smiling.

"You just name it, Poppa. I mean it, anything." Not two hours since the cops wrote their report and took the old man's statement, dragged Luís and Jaco to jail. Carlos getting away. Lenny thinking he had to find him before the cops did and make sure he stayed mum. Saying to the old man, "Thank God Paulina wasn't here." Lenny shaking his head, saying it like he meant it.

"Lenny, one thing . . ." Isaac dropped the smile.

"What's that?"

"Call me Poppa again, and I'm going to come over the counter and bust you in the chops too." Isaac reached in the drawer, took Luís's watch and set it on the glass, the sales tag dangling. Eyes on Lenny as he did it.

Looking from the watch to the old man, Lenny said, "What's this, a reward?"

"You did this."

Lenny finding it hard to hold the old man's eyes. "What are you saying, Poppa?"

And Isaac slapped him across the mouth.

Mouth dropping open, Lenny touched his face, then pulled it together. "Maybe you can jump a counter, old man, but you try that again . . ." Ready to take him apart.

"My girl wants a Get."

"You put her up to it, didn't you?" Lenny realized he was holding the side of his face, dropping his hand into a fist, thumping the counter glass. Wanted to take a swing at the old man.

"And you're going to give her one."

"Just like that?"

"She rates better than you, Lenny. I think even you know it."

"Not good enough for your little girl." Something between a laugh and a snort came out.

"You're not even close, Lenny."

"I were you, old man, I'd keep my nose in my own backyard."

Isaac tapped a finger on the watch.

"Heard about you old boys going off your nut, ready for the pasture. Go from jumping counters to needing diapers. Throwing tantrums like a second childhood."

Luís and Jaco fucked this up, the two coming in when Paulina wasn't here. Supposed to look like she got caught in a robbery gone wrong. Lenny's princess shooting off her mouth once too often. Leaving Lenny a widower, standing in black, with the family weeping and mourning. The rabbi reciting words about the Gates of Zion. Saw himself getting Mica to cater the shiva. All of it happening with no Get, Lenny keeping what was his.

"This time, Lenny, you're going to do the right thing."

"Or what, you go to the cops?"

"No cops, Lenny."

"You starting to believe the stories they tell about you, the ones you don't wanna talk about. Starting to believe your own legend." Lenny knowing all the stories: Isaac growing up in some part of Czechoslovakia that broke off, ended up being Hungary. An apprentice to a watchmaker until the shop was handed over to a nice Aryan family, Isaac's Mischling kin ending in the street with their yellow stars. No shoes and no food, learning to steal to survive, digging potatoes from the fields, eating them raw. Throwing stones for a gopher supper. Finally rounded up and sent to a camp. Put in two lines, the ones on the left going to work, the other line going to the showers, every man, woman and child handed a thin bar of soap.

Hard work became slave labor, going from bad to worse, to hell on Earth. Moved to a second camp, handed cups of thin soup passing for food, Isaac shrank week by week inside the gray stripes. Tugging the rope belt tighter every month to keep his pants on. The rags frayed and dirty, topped by the stench of death all around. Learning to chew his food slow, getting every bit of nutrition, living like that day by day, until the early months of '45, when Himmler handed the camp over without so much as a fight. The commander getting his SS boys burning the documents, then all of them fleeing in the night, out past the wall of death.

The first Allied jeeps rolled up to the outskirts of the camp, and jaws dropped at the sight inside the fences. Troops greeted by all the unburied dead, and those barely able to stand, all with their ribs showing, starving and sick, many dying from typhus. That's what welcomed the liberators. Stories Lenny had heard through the yenta grapevine, even before he dated Paulina, the tribe vowing never to forget, but Isaac going a different way, never saying a word about it.

"Yeah, you're one tough old goat, and I know your stories, old man, but you know what I do, at least you think you do — so you probably know I'm not somebody to fuck with." Lenny ignored the watch and turned for the door like he was tired of this.

"You know, Lenny, there's one story they don't tell . . ."

Lenny was at the door, not sure why he stopped, but he turned back.

"After the camp, I went to the sentencing, eleven guards answering for their crimes, all sent to Siberia. We called the commander the Belzeski beast. Him they hung by the neck for what he did. And Lenny . . ."

Lenny looked at the old man.

"I watched that trap door open under the beast, and you know something, I walked away on that day, the day I became a freier Mensch. Now, you wouldn't understand that, but understand this — you show at my door again, we sure won't need the cops. And it won't matter when you come, or about my age, or what I do in my pants." Smiling as he pressed the button, letting Lenny out.

Lenny turned and walked to the Galaxie, thinking the old man had it more than coming, same as Paulina. Took his key, noticed his shaking hand and wanting to smash his fist against the dash, instead fumbling the key into the ignition.

. . . rattus

Gabe's back ached from the cruel chair, handcuffed to the table leg, still forcing him to lean. The prosecuting asshole, Terrence Dow, stepped back into the interrogation room, Gabe's own lawyer leaving him in there to sweat.

Dow had gone to check the name Lenny Ovitz, finding he was a collector for Zimm, same as Gabe, a guy who took care of half of the collections in the Ward and ran all-night card games over in the Junction.

"This Lenny, just like you said, collections and cards. A small fish."

"Yeah, couldn't get a job at Eaton's and turned to crime." Gabe watched him sit, knowing he was after more than Lenny. He wanted Manni Schiller and Dag Malek, Ernie Zimm the cherry at the top. And if the Crown's man didn't know it already, he'd find out soon enough, Ernie Zimm could get to witnesses and make them unclear about what they saw. And he could get to him in holding too.

The cops had the gun, and Ernie's kid lawyer might cast some doubt, get a jury member to believe it was planted, have the right honorable fellow with the gavel rule out the greasy fingerprints on the pistol inside the poultry.

Gabe recalling the fingerprint examiner Ernie hired one time, got a manslaughter charge against Dag tossed out, the examiner disputing uniform standards, the number of identification points being light, talked about upholding the one dissimilarity doctrine, creating a cloud of doubt big enough for Dag to float out on.

And when it came time for jury selection, Ernie's people would pull a weak one from the herd, buy a head-shake of doubt. And Terrence Dow's case might go from a walk in the park to wobbling on its wheels. Yeah, Gabe Zoller had been around the block, working for a guy who knew how to play against the system. And there was the go-go girl alibi. But something wasn't feeling good about it. He watched Terrence Dow scrape back his chair and sit.

"So, you come to talk about some testi-money?" Gabe said.

Terrence Dow looked at him, saying, "Nice to see you hanging on to your sense of humor."

Gabe smiled at him, thinking if the two of them met in the dark of some street, and this schmuck looked at him like that, he'd be spitting teeth.

"Testi-money, that's good," Terrence Dow said. "Trouble with it, we've got the pistol, no doubt the one that killed the two innocents, with your prints all over it. Found the shells at the scene. Sure they'll match the grooves. Dug one from the plaster over the water cooler. Not to mention your prints all over the place. Got it all in safekeeping, not in some evidence locker."

"What happened to your safe place and my TV?"

"You remember the guy at the Market?"

"What guy's that?"

"A couple of his neighbors swear you stopped in and laid a beating on the man. Guess they're tired of you shaking down the block. You ask me, they're seeing it as a golden opportunity to be rid of your ass."

Gabe looked at this gassing attorney, still smiling.

"You know what, Gabe, I'm going to let you in on something, probably not what you expect . . ." Dow leaned over the table, his tie dangling down.

Gabe tempted to snatch the necktie and bang the man's head on the desk a couple times.

Dow leaned back like he read his mind, saying, "You're free to go."

Gabe blinked like he didn't hear him right, then squinted, trying to figure the game. Thinking his kid lawyer had been working behind the scenes, did it all without even showing up again. "You saying I made bail?"

"I'm saying you're free to go."

Gabe looked at him, then at his cuffed wrist.

"Soon as you sign the release." Dow nodded to the door, and the cop came in. Terrence Dow asking him to unhook Gabe, then setting his briefcase on the table, popping the latches.

"The hell you playing at?" Gabe said.

The cop removed the cuffs, then went to the door and stood holding it open. Dow set papers on the table, spun them and slid them across, pointed to where he wanted Gabe to sign. "Says you're on your own recognizance. You understand that word? Free to go, and aware of the risks."

Gabe looked at the cop, then at Dow. "The risks?"

"In case your people get the impression the two of us've been dealing. Trouble is, my higher-ups say no deal. The name you gave me, Lenny Ovitz. Yeah, he's of no interest. How it goes sometimes."

"He's the starter, like an appetizer."

"Yeah, I figured that when I ran the name — turns out the man's a total waste of time, too long a way from Zimm — the way my boss put it."

"So, like that, you're dropping the charges."

"We'll get back to you."

"One minute the bulls want to hang me, and you're telling me no parole. What the fuck's going on?"

Shrugging again, Terrence Dow pointed to where he wanted him to sign, clicked his pen and offered it.

Gabe signed his name and stood, rubbing at his wrist. "So I walk right out the door?"

The cop at the door held it open for him.

"And he plugs me trying to escape?"

Dow shook his head, good-natured, dropped the papers in his case and snapped it shut. "Not him you need to worry about, Mr. Zoller." Holding out his hand.

Gabe ignored the hand — his own palm feeling sweaty. Saying, "How about your witnesses, the gun with my prints, bullet in the plaster, all that?"

"You trying to build the case for me, Gabe?" Dow gave a grin, then started for the door.

"I want to see my lawyer." Gabe dropped back in the chair. "This is bullshit."

"You do what you want. You're free to go." Terrence Dow was out the door, his heels clicking down the hall, the cop still holding the door.

"I get it," Gabe leaned back. "I walk out, and Ernie figures me for a rat. You trying to get me clipped?"

"Save the taxpayers some money." The cop said, not looking at him.

Hearing the fading footsteps, Gabe jumped up. "Hey, hey! Hold up."

The footfalls stopped.

"Yes, Gabe?"

"I need a minute." Gabe knew he was being played, but he knew Ernie Zimm too.

The cop stayed at the door as the footsteps came back, Terrence Dow stepping back in the room, nodding for Gabe to sit, then sitting across from him, not wasting time now, dropping the nice-guy act. "I want names, and no more Lenny Ovitz. I want Schiller and I want Malek, and I want Zimm. Dates and places. Everything you got in that head. Am I being clear?"

"What do I get?"

"For one, you don't walk out that door. Two, I don't put you in gen-pop, let you get punked or shanked. And that's just for starters."

"So I give it all up, and you, what, shave off some time till parole?"

"I'll get you isolated, transferred out of province, a change of identity so your mother won't know you. Betting she wouldn't mind."

"Keep Momma out of it." Gabe frowned at the spot he was in, this guy twisting him around his finger. Saying, "No jail time, a new identity, and I need some cash, enough to get me gone."

Terrence Dow looked at the cop, and the two of them smiled like they just heard a good one.

"How much time we talking about?" Gabe said, folding his arms.

"Twenty-five with no way around it. You cooperate, and you'll see parole eligibility in . . . fifteen, maybe eighteen."

"Years? You know how old I'll be?" Gabe doing the math in his head.

"You want me having feelings for you, Gabe?"

"Ernie's got reach on the inside. I'll be looking over my back the rest of my life."

"Give me enough and he won't find you. I promise you that."

Gabe wiped at his forehead.

"Tell you what, talk to your lawyer if you want to go that way, the one Zimm's paying for, explore your options."

"Fuck you."

"You know, Gabe, I think you're getting the picture." Dow set his briefcase in front of him, took out a pad and pencil and slid them across. "Names, dates, places. And I know I said skip Lenny Ovitz, but toss him in — a show of good faith." He snapped his briefcase shut, got up and walked to the door. "I'll get them to send in some lunch. Be back at four. Give you time for memory lane. And don't worry about the spelling." And like that, Terrence Dow left Gabe looking at the paper.

The cop stepped out and let the door shut, locking it behind him.

Gabe yelling, "And my smokes. Don't forget my smokes — Mark Tens."

... *the flip side*

Paulina stood at the door, not making a move to let him in. Lenny took a glance back — nobody around, thinking he could do it now, standing on the stoop, this place not feeling like his anymore. Even called ahead this time, saying he wanted to come by for some of his stuff. Paulina saying he could come by if he didn't make a scene, made it sound like an appointment. She stepped aside and let him in.

The place looked the same, but it felt different. Frost coming off this woman he shared a bed with for two years. Lenny slipping off his shoes, something else he'd never done when he lived here, the tiles cold under his feet. The smile that used to light a room was gone, Paulina looking at him, giving him nothing. Lenny thinking of the fridge light coming on, not much light but plenty of chill. Used to talk about having kids, Lenny betting she took steps, making sure it never happened.

Yeah, he could do it now, the .32 out under the Galaxie's seat. Taking another look out to the street.

"I'm keeping the house." The first words out of her mouth, no debate in her tone.

"What happened to dividing the assets?" He glanced around, the living room and dining room suite, brass and crystal chandelier, all the stuff he'd paid for. The kingsized bed upstairs, dresser and mahogany night tables she had sent over from Italy. Her closet and half of his full of her clothes. "You forgetting who paid for it all?"

"You ever come home and not have a hot meal waiting? One I made after working all day?"

"Working part-time at your daddy's jewelry store."

"'Least it's honest work, Lenny."

"I can get a hot meal from a waitress. Leave a tip and I get a smile." He felt the anger rising inside.

"How about sex, ever do without it, I mean those times you came home?"

"Can tip for that too."

"You stayed out nights, didn't bother to call. My lawyer wants me seeing a doctor, thinks the stress of living with you is causing my migraines."

He caught himself from slapping her, lowering his tone, "You knew I was in the life — knew who I was."

"Listen to yourself, 'in the life.'"

"Way I remember, it turned you on."

"Till I got bored. Living with a cruel little boy putting on a show. Saving Mica from the same thugs who showed up at Poppa's. Who are you kidding, Lenny?"

And he slapped her, full across the mouth. Watched her reel back. And stopped himself from doing it again.

And she was on him — eyes like an animal — hammering at him with her fists, Lenny ducking and trying to catch her wrists. Caught the left one, got hit by the right — lost his grip, caught the other one, got hit again. Then he had both, squeezing her wrists as she squirmed, tried to kick, tried to bite. Paulina pulling close and bringing up her knee, Lenny twisting his own knees, trying to block it. Growling and gritting, she landed a head-butt. Lenny felt himself knocked back, catching himself against the hall table, the vase of flowers wobbling, water sloshing. Buckling, feeling Baby's teeth in his calf. Swinging a foot at the dog.

Turning back as she struck him with the vase. Feeling the water and stems washing over him. Lenny's head smacking the marble floor.

Putting his hands flat, he pushed up, heard that click, and stared up, Paulina with the two-shot derringer, the dog baring its teeth, fucking dog he fed the deli slices.

"Just for fun, Lenny ..." Catching her breath. "What's your idea of dividing the assets?"

He sat on the wet floor, shaking his head, seeing claw marks across the back of his hand, saying, "We talking about fair, or just your point of view?"

She laughed, shaking her head at him, her hair wild.

"Takes two to tango, Paulie."

"You, me, and your secrets. That's three, Lenny. Try to tango with that. And don't call me that."

"I can't talk about what I do, the things you don't want to know. We been all through that."

"Making it sound like you did me a favor."

"You know the people I work for. They even think you know something ..."

"So I ought to be grateful?"

"I'll give you the ten your old man gave us, plus some cash on top, say another ten. You can take your furniture, the car, the clothes, anything you came in with." His money had taken care of it all: the tennis club, the wardrobe, everything she sat her ass on. Working three days at her old man's jewelry store barely covered the groceries and utilities.

"Make it sound like I'm the one leaving," she said.

"You're dating a fuckin' cop!"

"A man who finds me interesting."

"Till he gets to know you." He got up slow, brushing at himself.

"Get out, Lenny ... or this will go off." Keeping the double barrels on him.

"Came for some of my stuff, or you want half of that too?"

Waving the gun, she said, "Wait outside, and I'll toss it out the window."

But he walked past her to the staircase. Baby growling, her topiary tail straight up.

"I'm warning you, Lenny."

Could be he'd catch a round in his back, right here in his own hallway, but he went up the stairs, doubting she would do it. Paulina following, keeping her aim. Saying, "Take what you want, but I'm putting the rest in the garage. You want it, come by on the weekend, after that I'm calling Goodwill. Last time you step in here."

In the bedroom, Lenny tore the bottom drawer out, let it drop to the shag carpet, grabbing a handful of Jockeys, realizing he had nothing to put it in. Looked at her with the peashooter in her hand. "Where's the suitcase?"

"With my travel stuff in it." Making no move to help him out.

"How about a trash bag, that be too much?"

She shifted to one leg, just stood looking at him.

Going to the ensuite, he upturned the wicker trash basket, dumping tissues and Q-tips on the floor, took the plastic liner and shoved his underwear in it, stepping over the drawer, getting some socks. Going to the double closet, folding his gray suit over his arm, he went past her down the stairs.

Paulina warning him again to come get the rest of his stuff Saturday. "Locksmith's coming after that."

"You get the house, and I get the blame. That about it?"

"Any way you want to tell it, Lenny. More than anything, I just want you out of my life."

Those cold eyes on him. Flicking a stem from his shoe, he slipped into the wet leather, turning for the door, and saying, "Somebody ought to explain to me why they call you the fair sex. Nothing fucking fair about it."

And she slammed the door.

Getting in the Galaxie, Lenny understood they were at stage four of marriage, should have known that back when the sex stopped, the discourse taking over when the woman stopped letting him between her legs. One thing, as long as they were married, she couldn't testify against him. There was that.

Tearing down the block and out of there, Lenny put a foot on the pedal, didn't bother with the stop signs. Having a conversation with the mirror, shaking his head, saying, "Cunt's seeing a lawyer." Laughing through a stop sign.

Somebody honked and he slapped his horn, the guy giving him the finger. Stopping in the lane, he reached under the seat as the other guy stopped and jumped out, coming with a ball bat. Rolling down the window, Lenny pointed the .32 at the son of a bitch, racking the slide. The guy turned, getting back in his car and speeding off.

He found himself east on Lawrence, the stop signs became traffic lights, Lenny not bothering with half of them, tearing around a bus in the oncoming lane, a long-haul flashing headlights at him.

"She gets the house, and I get the dive at the Empress." Lenny rabbit-punching the horn, his fingers strangling the wheel. His clothes wet against the vinyl seat. Thoughts of going over for the rest of his stuff, roll through her zinnias and tear up the lawn, take his key down the side of the stupid fake woodgrain on the Wagonaire. Pitch an edging brick through the bay window. Why not, he fucking paid for it all.

Getting a new image of this woman he used to call Schatzie. Hooking her manicured nails around the possessions, raking it in like winning at craps, leaving him a wreck. Whatever it had been, it wasn't anymore. Didn't matter he saved Mica that afternoon — a waste of time along with the money he paid the Portuguese. The woman running to the arms of a cop who was looking to lock Lenny up. And on top, Gabe Zoller was being held on murder charges. Everything turning to shit.

The old man had knocked Luís cold, catching Jaco in his mantrap doors. Paulina's cop bound to figure it was the same guys who tried robbing Mica. Luís and Jaco would give him up in a heartbeat. Lenny with his balls in a vice, with Paulina cranking the handle — acting like he ought to be lucky to get out with his socks and underwear.

He had to keep her from talking to the lawyer or the cop. Should have ended at the house, but he'd plan it and get it done right. Tromping the pedal, Lenny blew through another amber, feeling the rushing air on the cold sweat. Yeah, she had to go, but first, he had to go see Carlos. All of it had to happen without Ernie Zimm hearing about any of it.

The flashing cherry in the rearview got his attention. Goddamn unmarked cop car, the Plymouth roaring up behind him. First thought was to bolt, but the cop had made his plate, be an easy call for back-up.

He eased to the shoulder and shut it off, watching the guy step out behind him. Not a uniformed cop, this guy taking his shield from his belt as he came to Lenny's window, tapping the tin against the window.

Lenny cranked the window and glanced up. "I help you, officer?" Smiling at Paulina's cop.

The guy stood looking down at him. "Bad day, Lenny?"

"Makes you say that?" Lenny thinking of the .32 under the seat.

"You're kinda wet."

"You never go swimming in your clothes?"

"They got medication these days . . ."

"Giving curbside medical advice, huh?"

Gary Evans tucked the shield away, looking out ahead, then back down at him. "Followed you from the house — doing sixty in a thirty, blew through I don't know how many signs, along with a couple of lights."

"So write a bunch of tickets."

"Couldn't leave it alone, huh? The woman wants you out of her life."

"Just the tickets, and spare the Dear Abby."

And Gary Evans stepped close and socked him in the mouth.

Knocked across the console, Lenny's hand scrambled under the seat.

Gary had his door open and was pulling him out before he could reach it.

"You want dating advice, just say so." Lenny was out and shoved him off, caught him with a hook. "Well, one thing, she's not fussy for tongue. Maybe you already found —" And Gary swung again, Lenny ducking it, catching most of it on his shoulder, coming back with a good cross.

"We gonna dance, how about you lose the piece?" Lenny said, jabbing a couple of times, eager to put a beating on this cop.

And Gary pulled the holstered piece, and the badge, and set them on Lenny's hood. Then came rushing in, Lenny catching him under the ribs, following it with a chopping left, the cop stumbling back.

"Seeing a man's wife. What's the matter, you can't get your own?" Jabbing, catching Gary in the mouth. Missing with the right.

Gary coming under it, slamming his fist into Lenny's ribs, knocking him against the Galaxie's door, hammering in one more and pushing off. Winded, he reached a sap from his pocket, saying, "We met playing singles. The girl's got backswing, I can tell you that. And you know, I think I'm helping her game."

"Didn't mention about being club champ, two years running?" Lenny stood looking at the sap.

Gary was grinning like he didn't believe it, standing ready.

"Could be she figures a goy cop's got an eggshell ego."

"That's bullshit, club champ."

"Two years running." Lenny shrugged and shook his head, enjoying this.

"A wife like that, and you an errand boy for Zimm. Go figure." Gary shook his head.

"No crime selling cruises. A thousand bucks gets you Miami, a nice cabin, the dinner-show package, and any luck you catch Jackie Gleason, maybe Mel Tormé."

"Love that guy, the Velvet Fog."

"We done?" Lenny grinned.

"You're looking at seven-to-ten, Lenny." Gary Evans dropped the sap in his pocket, holstered the pistol and clipped on the badge.

"Gonna let my attorney know, you're banging the wife of the guy you're trying to nail."

"What I love about you guys, cracking wise and acting tough, and never seeing the train coming. Or, maybe you didn't hear, we got your pal Zoller on a double homicide."

"The whole town's heard."

"But did you hear, you're the first one he gave up."

... *the canary*

"He's a dead man." Ernie's voice boomed through the place. The slam of the phone, something smashing inside the office.

Manni Schiller looked at Dag Malek, sitting in the outer office, saying, "Think that's the last mug." Getting up from his desk, he went to Ernie's door, ready to duck in case he was wrong.

Ernie looking up from behind the desk. "The fucker's singing."

"Gabe?"

"Who the fuck we talking about?" Ernie looked out the window, the view to the alley in back, his Riviera parked on an angle, its bumper against the trash cans. "The dumb fuck."

Manni stood waiting, then saying, "Say what you want done."

Ernie looked at him. "Cohen went to meet the prosecutor. Guy was a no-show. So he goes back to holding, but our boy won't see him. Like he's suddenly got better things to do — like giving us up."

"You sure?"

"He coughed up Lenny. Heard it from the guard." Picking the lamp off the bureau, Ernie hefted it, looked at the Eiffel Tower print hanging crooked on the paneled wall, thought better of it and set it back down.

Manni thinking of a couple of Junction boys doing a stretch in the Don, along with a bull they had on the inside. Two of them to do the shanking, the other looking away.

"Take care of it, and get Dag to book me a holiday," Ernie said, still looking out. "Ester says Rome's good this time of year."

"Yeah, Rome's the place." Going back to his desk, Manni looked at Dag. "Man wants to take the wife, show her the Colosseum."

Dag nodded, getting the picture, frowning about it.

"Gonna get 'brainless fuck' chiseled on his headstone." Manni picked up his phone, dialed and waited, talking low, saying, "You know who it is?" Waited and then, "And why I'm calling?" Then saying, "Let me know when it's done." And he hung up, looked up past the line of clocks, then back at Dag.

Looking at a guidebook, Dag said, "High eighties, sunny skies. La Dolce fucking Vita."

Something else smashed in the office.

"Hotel del Sole, got a nice day tour, good restaurants and plenty of statues Ernie can bust up."

Manni nodded, saying, "Get Lenny to do the drop — and make sure he knows Gabe gave him up."

"You want a coffee?" Dag pushed up, went to the table, looking at the empty pot on the warmer, the empty dish-rack where the mugs were kept. Saying he was going across the street. Right under the window, the cops keeping surveillance, peeking out the window, snapping long-lens photos, Dag hoping they got his good side.

Manni picked up the phone and called Lenny's place. Getting his wife, Paulina, who told him she had no idea where the louse was and didn't care, then told him not to call again and hung up. Manni looked at the dead line, saying, "Guess the honeymoon's over."

. . . lying in wait

Gary had parked across from the parkette, kept an eye on Paulina's place for a while, making sure she was alone before knocking. No ex-husband around this time, unless he was hiding in the closet.

"You teach science, huh?" Paulina said, seeing the welt on his face. "Tough subject."

"Yeah well, guess I bent the truth."

"Bent it?"

"I left a couple things out, and I don't feel good about it. Fact, I'm glad it's out, a load off my mind."

"Well, good for you, Gary."

"Look, it started out being the job, then we got to playing and getting to know each other, and . . ."

"And you lied, Gary."

"Yeah, and I'm sorry for it, and hoping we can get past it." Looking at her, wanting her to see the good guy past the lies.

"You wanted to nail my ex, and figured why not nail me while you're at it."

"Was never like that."

"But you thought I knew what he's into?"

"You know what I was thinking? That you married the wrong guy."

"So by lying, what, you were saving me from a guy like that? You see where I might have a problem?"

"You can take care of yourself, I know that, Paulina."

"And the whole time thinking you'd get me in bed."

"Not the whole time."

"But it crossed your mind."

"Well, I won't lie to you — well, anymore. I promise."

"So I should be flattered?" Stepping closer, touching the back of her fingers to his red cheek, liking him off balance, this tough cop she could whip at singles, saying, "It crossed your mind, like how many times?"

Looking into those smiling eyes, realizing she was playing again, his heart kicking as she leaned close, put her hand around the back of his neck. Her mouth close to his, saying, "Come on, how many times?"

Forgetting he was on the job, saying, "Every time I look at you."

"Uh huh. So, what happened to your face?"

"Hazards of the job." Gary feeling her breath on his neck.

"There you go again, leaving something out." Her finger playing with the back of his ear. "You want to know what I was thinking the first time you asked me to play?"

"What's that?"

And she drew back, looking serious. "Thought if I beat you in straight sets, could you take it."

"You're cute." And he tried to kiss her.

Paulina putting a hand to his chest, holding him back.

"Already found out you're the ladies' champ."

"You knew?"

"I'm a cop, Paulina; I know all kinds of things." Smiling, then trying again to kiss her, keeping himself from lying more.

"So, you up for a rematch, maybe make it interesting this time?" Paulina looking in his eyes, not pulling away.

"You bet."

"I'll think about it." She nudged him back, shutting the door, leaving him standing there feeling dumb.

. . . *kitty punchers*

Lenny was telling himself it was part of the job, one more thing Ernie Zimm wanted done. Gabe wasn't a bad collector; a little nuts, but that came from doing the job a long time. They were partners on the tenement block, had good times when they hit the Yonge strip after their collections, catching the Hawk, Little Caesar or Chad Allan doing a set at Le Coq d'Or, Olympic Bowling right upstairs. Gabe "The Twist" Zoller showing Lenny his pick-up moves on the goy pussy that floated in after their storefront jobs. Lenny remembering the two women sitting at the bar next to their table, saying they came for drinks and good music and not for bad company. It's how the one with the cropped haircut and hoop earrings explained it to Gabe.

Gabe shrugged like it was her loss, looked to her friend, and said, "How about you, sugar, up for some fun?"

"I'm sure you're a swell guy, really, but how about you go screw off?"

Gabe called them the type who feared a good high hard one, sat back unfazed and ordered a couple more pints. When the waitress set the glasses down, he turned back to the ladies and said, "Last chance to ride my Catalina."

The women got up and left their half-finished drinks on the bar and walked out.

Gabe telling Lenny his car seats could melt away the panties on anything but that kind, calling them kitty punchers.

Lenny guessed Gabe Zoller didn't always strike out that bad; he wasn't awful-looking, just had an out-of-date way of selling it. Gabe saying he had better luck at the Elmo, or with the cowboy crowd at the Horseshoe, honest women in jeans and bandannas coming to hear Little Jimmy or the Tysons.

Lenny was wondering what happened to his partner, a guy he'd just seen that morning, kicking out the squatters from one of the buildings. Lenny facing it, Gabe had screwed the pooch, and screwed it bad — laying a beat-down on one of the chicken-sellers in the Market, letting his temper off the leash in broad daylight. Then driving to the fur district, double-parking in the witnesses and capping the Merchant of Mink, along with the bookkeeper. And this from a man who knew the rules as well as anybody in the life: you boil over and cost the outfit, and a guy like Ernie Zimm's going to brand you a liability. And getting busted then ratting on the outfit meant you paid for your sins.

They sent Lenny to make the drop, cash in the envelope to pay the Junction boys inside to take care of Gabe. Not sure why Ernie didn't send somebody else, worried he got wind the two of them bought the dives by St. James Town, borrowing heavy from Ungerman — not a guy Ernie got along with. Or the boss was still pissed about the shootout with the Italians early in the year, the time Gabe took a bullet, bringing heat on the outfit.

Lenny got out of his car and went up the precinct stairs, passed a couple of uniforms going out the door. Stepping through the inner wood-and-glass doors, he checked along the paneled hallway, the place smelling of pork and pain. A couple more uniforms talking at the far end of the hall. Lenny went to the desk sergeant, asked if he was O'Riordan, a big Irish mug with deep lines across his forehead.

"Who else would I be?" The man put his boozy eyes on Lenny, cheeks like a bulldog. "You one of Zimm's?"

Lenny slid the envelope on the desk like Dag had told him, doing it in plain sight. The sarge muttered something about the way Lenny looked at him, like he was better than him. He pawed the envelope, making it disappear. Lenny turned and walked back out, betting the sarge was reaching in the bottom drawer of the beat-up counter for his flask.

Getting his mind back on his own troubles, thinking it was time to find Carlos, he wondered what it would cost him this time, keep the three Portuguese quiet, two of them in custody, the third running off. Lenny getting into his own deep end.

... *a drop off the map*

The bull locked Gabe's cell door and walked off. This fucking place smelling of sweat, piss and criminals. Gabe hearing the footfalls fade, his eyes adjusting to the gloom, the double bunk, the stained toilet with no lid in the corner. Setting the folded blanket and the excuse for a pillow on the bottom bunk, he turned to the snoring shape on the top.

"Hey, buddy." He slapped a hand at the mattress, waited and did it again.

The shape shifted and grunted. "The fuck's your problem?"

"You're in my spot."

"Fuck you." The man rolled to the concrete wall, his back to Gabe.

The voice belonging to a big son of a bitch, meaning Gabe had to make it count, setting his feet and grabbing man and blanket, yanking and getting out of the way.

The guy crying out as he tumbled and hit the floor, then Gabe was kicking before he could get untangled. Tearing into him with his feet, Gabe kept going.

The man throwing up his arms, trying to deflect, pawing at him, but Gabe kept chopping, not giving the man a chance.

Somebody yelled from the cell across, but Gabe kept it up. Finally stopping, he put his hands on his knees, catching his wind. And when he could, he said, "I'm top dog, you get that?"

Bleeding from the mouth, the man sat up, trying to get his feet untangled from his blanket.

"You want more, it's okay by me," Gabe said.

The guy put up his hand, no fight in him now.

"There we go, not so hard, right?" Gabe backed to the bars, thought he might throw up on the man, trying not to show it.

The big man was hunchbacked with a few years and fifty pounds on him — slow getting to his feet, he took his pillow off the top, then flopped onto the bottom bunk, groaning something about his ribs feeling busted.

Gabe waited, then hoisted himself up on top, knowing if he had to do time in this shit-hole, he had to let the yard know who he was. Crazier than the next guy. A tall order in a place like the Don, Gabe counting on word getting around fast.

Folding his hands behind his head, he listened to the sounds from the corridor, the rasping from the bunk below, the guy in the next cell talking in his sleep, another guy down the line crying. He couldn't see the shapes in the cell across the hall, but it sounded like two men going at it, grunting and whispering, trying to be quiet about it.

The Crown's man, Terrence Dow, wasn't lying about him doing time. Gabe knew there was no way around it. But working a deal meant a softer landing than the Don, and maybe a reduced sentence. Stupid to let loose like that, popping the mink guy and the broad with the wig. The goddamn business with Lenny setting him off, Gabe not believing how dumb he'd been letting Lenny talk him into buying in on the block of slum buildings, getting in debt up to his neck with Ungerman.

When he got his release, he had to be a new man on the outside, meaning a new identity. Lying there, he played around with a new identity, thinking of names of movie stars, coming up with Marlon, James, Rock, and Burt, but nothing that fit him.

Chet sounded down-home, belonging on a guy who dug Ian and Sylvia — Tyson with his golden voice and his woman with the knockers all over the place — Gabe loved that tune about the loving sound.

Yeah, Chet fit him. And he came up with Mullins. Chet Mullins. And he let it roll off his tongue. Chet Mullins sounded down-home and goy all the way through. The kind of name belonged on a guy who got the top bunk, and not a name that hinted he belonged to the tribe, something he'd been wanting to shake since he was back in grade school. He hung his hand over the side, snapped his fingers and said, "Hey brother, you still up?" Snapped a couple more times, the snoring turning to sputters, then a grunt.

"The name's Chet. You hearing me?"

"What?"

"Chet Mullins, case you want to know."

"That you, Chet, huh?" The voice heavy with sleep and swollen lips.

"That's right, Chet Mullins." Gabe liking the handle.

"Well, uh, good to meet you, Chet."

Gabe thinking he'd get the Crown-clown Terrence Dow to work up a new ID, get him relocated to anyplace but here. All the dirt he had on Zimm's people was going to spell his early release. And he wasn't feeling too bad about it. Maybe Lenny didn't have it coming, in spite of talking him into that apartment block. The pile of shit would land on Ernie

Zimm, and Gabe didn't care about that. Zimm keeping him on collections since catching the bullet after they took out the Italians, protecting Zimm's turf. Now Zimm was sending him a kid lawyer, promising him a go-go dancer — Gabe having no confidence after Terrence Dow threatened to let him walk, making it look like he took a deal.

Gabe would hold out for a lighter sentence, then he'd become Chet, grow a mustache, and he'd color his hair light, let the sideburns go Glen Campbell, to the bottom of his ears. And jeans instead of slacks, a T-shirt, and one of those Levi jackets with the brass buttons. No shirt and tie for old Chet Mullins.

Worst part, he'd have to give up the Catalina. That car had been his signature ride, the V8 with the overhead valves, dual Thrush pipes, the hydramatic tranny. Shame of it, it was a beacon, everybody in the Ward knowing that black ride coming down the block. As much as he hated the thought, he'd get the landlady to sell it, tell her to get what she could for it and hold the money for him. When Gabe got out as Chet, he'd collect and get himself behind the wheel of a pickup, something like a four-eyed Dodge. A bench seat with the AM dialed to country and western. Then he'd slip out of that flop, tell the landlady he'd call her sometime, then blow out of town forever.

Winnipeg was west, a place of ice and snow and rednecks. West of there was nothing but grain silos, a fucking rodeo, until you hit the coast, and nothing there but rain and draft dodgers. Vancouver on the wrong side of the mountains. The other way was Ottawa, the starch-in-the-collar town of lying assholes and pencil-pushers, not a place for a guy named Chet Mullins driving a Power Wagon. Montreal might be alright for a while, except for speaking the wrong language. He heard there was night action, and the French pussy — he'd heard good things. Past that lay Nova Scotia, the land of lobster and more nothing. Dartmouth and Halifax might be good for lying low, places where Ernie Zimm had no reach.

Terrence Dow wanted Ernie Zimm bad enough, meaning he'd pop out the big government tit and let Chet have a good suck. Gabe playing with the idea of doing short time in a medium joint, slipping away upon his release, getting in the Dodge, do his lying low, then drive south until he ran out of land. Use what was left of the tit money and set up a bar, some straw-roof place on a Key West beach, sell Michelob and screw tanned tourist pussy under a big sunset. Another place Ernie Zimm wouldn't come looking.

Thinking about women in bikinis when he heard footfalls coming along the corridor. The bull on his rounds, his flashlight intruding into the cell, saying, "New guy, you good?"

"I'm good, boss." Lying awake, he wondered what the fuck was taking Dow moving him out of here. No doubt, the Crown's man had a yard of shit to wade through getting Gabe his deal, but the lawyer had to know he was dead meat in this place, soon as Ernie Zimm figured him for a rat. As the bull's footfalls faded, he had a thought that had him bolting up, feeling the cold wet forming under his armpits. Then whispering into the dark, "Hey, my bud, you still up?" Waiting, then kicking a leg down on the stained mattress that had seen too many inmates on top of it, saying, "Hey bud, you hearing me?"

"Goddamn you got against a man getting his rest?" The voice rousing from sleep.

"Think I might'a found Jesus."

"Right in the east wing, huh? Well, good on you, brother. Give him my regards."

"The savior's been giving me shit."

"That so?"

"Wants me mending fence, on account of my temper getting loose — like the way I did you."

"Don't sweat it, brother. I heal good. Be forgotten by morning."

"No, I done you poor, and I got to set it right." Gabe swung his legs over the side and hopped down, looking in at the man.

"I don't dish, and I don't want nothing from you, man."

"You think I'm a fag? Jesus, look at yourself ... What I'm doing, I'm giving you back your bunk. Took what wasn't mine, the kind of thing landed me here in the first place. Now I got Jesus saving my mind, telling me I got to turn a new leaf. Giving it back."

"If it's all the same, just let a man catch his rest, will ya?"

"Look pal, you argue with me all you want, but this is Jesus ..."

"Come on, man, a bunk's a bunk."

"Are we gonna have more fuckin' trouble?" Gabe getting set to drag the man out again.

"Okay, okay." The hunchback put his feet to the concrete, muttering.

"Bad mojo arguing with Christ." Bundling his blanket, the nest of lice, then grabbing his jailhouse pillow. Gabe told him again he was Chet, offering his hand.

"Okay, Chet, I'm Dice." The big man looked at the extended hand like he didn't trust it, then shook it.

"How'd you get that handle, Dice? You gamble?" Gabe making small talk, watching the man grabbing the side and hoisting himself up. The big man telling he got the name on account of his hands shaking, what the prison doc chalked up to an overactive thyroid.

"That a catching thing?" Gabe wiping his hand on his pants.

"Naw, you got no worries. Just the glands working double time. Kicks my heart in a higher gear is all."

"That's the shits."

"Yeah, you might say."

"Well, 'least it's not catching. So, look, was good to meet you, Dice. And sorry about going off on you. Likely got a condition or two of my own. But, with Jesus, things'll clear up."

Getting settled back on top, Dice said, "Got a fine service Sundays, I mean if you're seeking the Lord."

"Good to know, yeah, I'll look him up." After a few minutes, Gabe heard Dice back to sawing logs. Thinking he ought to feel bad for what could be coming. And he lay in the dark, his hands behind his head and his ears pricked up. After a while, he propped up to keep himself from drifting off. And he just listened and waited.

A half hour more before he heard a scuff, could be the bull coming back on his rounds, maybe bringing Dow with him this time, getting Gabe out of there, middle of the night. Something Ernie Zimm wouldn't expect.

Then came another scrape, then a whisper. Sitting up, he leaned forward to get a look out the bars, hearing Dice's rasping up above. Then shadows showed along the corridor, and he curled to the concrete wall, tugging the blanket over his head. And he was thinking about Jesus, wondering if it was something Chet Mullins might put his faith in. Get one of those crosses for around his neck, the ones church folk wear.

He felt them more than heard them. The light scrape of metal on metal as the door opened, and in they came. And he held his breath, trying to count how many, forcing himself to stay turned to the wall, his ears growing ten sizes in the dark. Tensing for a blade in the back.

There was a thump, a slap and a muffled cry.

Somebody whispering, "Hey, rat."

Another thump as Dice was yanked back to the floor. Several men stomping like they were in a hurry, far worse than what Gabe had done to him. Then they stood him up, then thunking sounds and moans, muffled by hands over the man's mouth. Gabe knowing he was hearing shanks going in, thinking of the beef hanging at Canada Packers. Then the sounds of Dice being dragged out. The door shutting easy behind them. And they were gone.

Gabe didn't turn from the wall for a long while. Wide awake when the guard came by about a half hour later, the bull whistling softly, checking the lock on the cell door, then walking off on his rounds.

. . . meet navalha

L enny walked in back of the Lisbon Club, taking his time, going along the hall of black-and-white sports photos: Seleção Portuguesa de Futebol; the Volta a Portugal; touradas of Vila Franca de Xira; and the Grand Prix at Circuito da Boavista. Going past closed doors and into the barroom, Tiffany lamps giving a green glow to the place. The same bartender behind the bar, fixing drinks for the only couple, sitting at a table by the front window, locked in their world of conversation. The barman took the glasses and set them on their table, going back behind his bar. Rows of bottles on glass shelves. A couple of draft taps in front of him. Stepping to the bar, Lenny waited for him to look up. Yeah, he knew who he was. Lenny saying, "Where is he?"

"Don't know nobody." The guy put his big hands on the bar, his sleeves rolled up.

"Carlos."

The man shook his head. "Não falo inglês."

"How about this, that drink you made, you know the one?"

The guy twisted his mouth in a grin.

"What was in it?"

"Something to make you shit."

"Laxative?"

"One like a bomb."

"Figured that's funny, huh?"

"Think so, yeah." The guy looking at Lenny like what was he going to do about it.

"That a clip-on?" Lenny nodded at the tie hanging from the white shirt, this guy with his sleeves rolled up.

The guy glanced down, and Lenny caught hold and gave a yank, drawing the .32 with the other hand, pressing it to the man's neck, the man's hand trying to fumble under the bar. Lenny jerked the tie harder, and he stopped.

"Put it on the bar." Kept a grip on the tie.

With his head cocked, the man set a revolver on the bar top, held his hands out.

"Point with your nose . . ."

The man nicked his head to the back hall, the doors Lenny passed on the way in.

"Which one?"

"Last one on the right."

"In there alone?"

"Just him."

"Any surprise and I shoot you, your own gun."

"Just him."

"Fix me two of your bombs, same as before." Lenny kept the .32 on him, pocketed the revolver.

"You want to shit?"

"Big and steamy."

The guy looked at the pistol, then went about fixing the drinks, taking a packet of powder, dumping half in each glass.

"Make 'em doubles." Lenny meaning the powder.

"Then you taste it."

"I don't mind." Lenny waited for him to set the drinks down, watching him use a plastic swizzle, mixing them up. "Bottoms up." Lenny slid a glass toward him, wagging the pistol when the guy shook his head and refused, finally racking the slide.

The guy considered, frowned, then he sipped.

"All of it." Lenny waiting till it was gone, then he picked up the other glass, and he started down the back hall, saying, "You holding anything but a bar rag when I come out, you won't get to shit yourself. You get me?"

The guy gave a nod.

The glass in one hand, his .32 in the other, Lenny stepped to the back, past the photos, and pushed open the door on the right, the room lit by a TV screen.

"Olá, Carlos." Same fucking game on.

Turning his head, Carlos was coming up with the razor in his fist.

Dashing the drink at him, Lenny sidestepped the swishing steel, and he fired, missed with the first shot, killing the TV, and he fired again.

Carlos stumbled back, caught it in the gut, and folded into the chair he'd been sitting in, looking down at himself like he didn't believe he'd been shot, then he dropped to the floor in a fetal curl, a dark stain spreading on the floor.

"Your team's gonna lose." Lenny shot him in back of the head, turned and stepped to the door, careful sticking his neck out, looking to the bar. The couple and the bartender were gone. Lenny going out the back door. No way he could get to Luís and Jaco in lock-up, but guessing they'd get word, and they'd think twice about talking, guessing Ernie Zimm had people on the inside.

. . . half moon of hell

T he uniforms led him out the back way, Gabe's hands in cuffs. Gabe squinting into the morning light. Seeing two men escorted from the back of a wagon, hands in cuffs, being led into the door he was coming out of, a familiar look about the arrested men. One cop putting him in back of the squad car, the other getting behind the wheel, driving from the old Don.

"My buddy Dow send you?" Gabe hating his hands cuffed, not sure if Terrence Dow sent them, having him moved. Could be Ernie's guys, realizing they shanked the wrong guy last night, taking him someplace where the shots wouldn't be heard.

He got no answer. From the back seat, he watched the Parkway roll past, the cruiser turning onto Yonge and heading north, crossing the 401, then the 7, the two cops finally talking to each other about the Leafs and the chances with Mahovlich, Keon and Armstrong. Talking hockey in June, months before the start of the season. Not a word about the killing at the Don last night, Dice having pancakes with Jesus this morning, passing the butter and syrup. Betting the big man was free of that shaking in his hands.

Leaning to the seat-back, Gabe tried to get into the talk, "You boys forgetting about Eddie Shack?"

They glanced at each other and ignored him, the driver going on about Red Kelly, the other saying it would be up to Tim Horton, both liking that Bower was in net.

"Any way you look at it, they got a shot at the Cup, no doubt in my mind," the driving cop said.

"You got it right, brother." Didn't matter what Gabe said, these putzes weren't talking to him, acting like they'd catch something if they did.

The city turned to the suburbs, bricks and mortar becoming open fields, asphalt to gravel, the funk of manure. A half an hour from the Don, Gabe still not sure who these guys were working for. Fearing they'd pull to the side, drag him out and finish what the inmates were sent to do last night. A sign flew past: *Welcome to Aurora*. Felt like taps leaking under his arms as they blew by another sign, some-place called Goodwill.

Finally the tires bit onto the gravel lot of a roadside joint called the Half Moon, a rundown four-story with a faded hotel sign out front, an add-on looking like a dining room. Didn't look like any customers were in the place.

A couple of tree-shrouded buildings up the road hinted this could be a town. The blond cop behind the wheel turned, the hard look of the guy who played *The Rifleman*, saying to Gabe, "Here we are."

The other one getting him out of the back and leading him through the door marked *Office*.

The manager stood behind the counter in overalls, had a hook for a nose, a neck like a llama, nodding like he expected them, didn't bother him that Gabe was in cuffs, saying, "You must be the Nash party?"

The blond cop said, "And this here's our guest of honor, James Nash." Nudging Gabe with a shoulder. Then taking off the bracelets so Gabe could sign in, getting registered. Gabe scribbling Chet Mullins, thinking of the odds, stabbing the cop with the Bic, fighting the other one for his gun, then making a run for it without getting shot in the back. But it was getting clear, these cops were working for Terrence Dow. Meaning, he was safe for now.

The cop who'd ridden shotgun on the way up got behind the wheel and drove off, Gabe being escorting to the top floor. Saying to the blond cop, "So, when do I eat?"

The cop opened the door to the room at the top of the stairs and shoved him in.

Gabe looked around, saying, "Guess you're not expecting a tip."

The cop shut the door behind him.

"Hey, you didn't point out the features." Looking at the bed, a side table and a beat-up dresser, three drawers with two knobs missing. "Joint looks like Keon's been taking slap shots." The smell of mothballs and neglect. What wasn't faded was stained, a threadbare sheet over a spineless mattress. Going to the window, he tried to push it up, guessing it had been nailed or painted shut. A thin blanket lay folded on the end of the bed. The lone pillow looked like he could bang dander from it, reduce it to half its size. Still, an upgrade from the one in the Don. And nobody trying to shank him.

The cop spoke through the door, "Can's at the end of the hall. Tap if you got to go. Give an extra minute 'cause I got to put the cuffs back on."

"Yeah, meaning you're gonna shake me off."

The cop opened the door, smiled as he shot a fist into Gabe's gut, folded him over his knees. Gabe trying not to toss up last night's chow.

"That's how I do it, shake the drops," the cop said, shutting the door, adding, "Anything else you need, just let me know. Be right outside, tend to your every need."

Gabe heard the key turn in the lock, then the chair creaked under the cop's weight. Thinking he used to take a punch like that, counter with a rocket to the jaw and flatten his opponent.

Terrence Dow was one cheap prick, sticking his star witness in this out-of-the-way dump, the only amenity was gestapo outside the door, using him like an Everlast bag. He looked out the window, four floors down to the gravel lot. The neon sign claiming they had vacancies. This whole town with a vacancy look about it, not a soul in sight.

Sitting on the bed, Gabe watched a bank of clouds rolling and changing shapes. Something he hadn't done since he was a kid. Then he switched on the tube angled from the corner of the room. The decade-old RCA box in black-and-white glory took forever to warm up, the tubes glowing from the back of the set. Rabbit ears on top.

Moving the ears around, Gabe worked them to get the least amount of snow. *Wayne & Shuster* on 6, *Littlest Hobo* on 9. He went with the dog, a rerun of the shepherd trotting to a new town, finding some bullied boy in need of a friend, the kid trying to adopt him in the end, and the dog walking off, the way he always did while the dumb theme played. Gabe guessed the way they filmed it, it was supposed to jerk some tears. And he had to admit, he had a liking for that dog. Wondered why he never got one of his own, supposed to be man's best friend. Not like he had any real friends. Wasn't close with the landlady, the only person other than

Lenny in his life. Things went okay with her as long as he paid his room rent on time. Sometimes he caught a drink or two of whiskey with her on the front porch, once in a blue moon when they had more than a couple he put a hand up under her housecoat. Once or twice it led to sex in her room. Another time it happened right on the front porch, under the shawl she kept across her knees. The woman wasn't much, the booze wearing away whatever looks she once had, but on those occasions she was eager enough, and never hit him up for more money.

His lunch came near two, a slice of pimento loaf on white, with a smear of Parkay and a streak of mustard, along with a bottle of Tahitian Treat. Opening the bread slices, he decided since Parkay wasn't butter, and the pimento loaf likely wasn't made of real meat, he considered the sandwich pareve enough — a force of habit — and he ate it, and it sure beat what they slopped up at the Don's chow hall last night — not something Chet Mullins was going to worry about from here on. The bottle felt like it had been left in the sun. And no opener.

Banging the pop top off on the corner of the dresser, Gabe sat on the bed, some of the pop fizzing and dripping down his hand and onto the floorboards. Flushing down his lunch, he bunched the pillow and propped himself against the wall, watching Dr. Who and his granddaughter meet a bunch of fake-looking aliens on some fake-looking planet, supposed to be deep space. Getting caught up in the story line, Gabe put off going to the can, nearly wet himself by the final commercial, swung his feet off the bed and knocked on the door, waited, then banged on it. Footfalls came up the stairs, the cop growling a warning about him pounding on the fucking door.

Gabe saying he was about to spray the walls.

"What are you, five?" The cop opened the door, gave him a scowl and took his time leading him down the hall, no cuffs, telling Gabe to wash his hands after.

Gabe called through the door about there being no soap. No hot water or towel either.

"They got soap back at the Don, can have you there by supper. Your boyfriend'll be happy to toss it down in front of you."

Flushing the toilet, Gabe checked the tiny window. Could open it a couple of inches, but there was no way to squeeze out of there. Plus, it was four flights straight down with no tree or lower roof to break the fall. He opened the door and stepped out, saying, "Something else to do around here but watch TV?"

"Be glad you got that." The cop taking him back to his room, walking behind him, poking him in his lower back with the nightstick.

"Yeah, two channels. A man can't want more than that. Hey, you see a *Globe* or *Star* around, wouldn't mind catching up on the world. Don't care if it's a week old. And a *TV Guide*'d be good."

"Like you can read." The cop shoved him back into the room.

"You see my man Dow, tell him his accommodations are top notch. Howard Johnson all the way."

The cop bunched his fist and hit him in the middle again, shut the door and turned the key in the lock, then sat on the chair outside.

He'd been ready that time and tightened his abs. Gabe dropped back on the bed and let the pain subside, falling asleep to *Telepoll*. Didn't remember changing the channel, waking to Don Messer working his fiddle with Marg and Charlie, doing "Rubber Dolly." Looking out the window again — not a cloud in the late-afternoon sky — shadows doing a long creep from the cornstalks across the two-lane. Shutting off the TV on account of the heat coming off the tubes in back, raising the temperature in the room by a half dozen degrees. No ceiling fan, the thin curtains no match for the summer sun beaming into the room.

Gabe sat by the cracked window open all of two inches, hoping for any kind of breeze. Once a rusty pick-up, from the time of Diefenbaker, smogged past, its engine backfiring, sounding like a gunshot. The highlight of the afternoon.

Guessing by the shadows on the road, it was nearing six when he pounded on the door again, risking another punch to the gut, Gabe sweating like a bear, demanding to see a menu.

The fresh cop on duty made the same crack about him being able to read.

"You clowns need a new joke book."

The cop told him supper was coming anytime now. Warned him about banging on the door again.

"Yeah, sorry to wake you," Gabe said.

How did this dump of a hotel survive? Nothing around but the faded restaurant sign: no gas station, no church steeple, no sound of kids playing, not a schoolhouse or barn in sight, not even a crossroad nearby. Just the gravel one running north and south past miles of corn. If Ernie Zimm sent somebody, Gabe would know when the million crickets stopped chirping.

At the next change of the guard, he was handed a pad and pen, along with word from Dow, Gabe told to write down anything else that came to his mind: names, dates and places. Terrence Dow wanting to show the higher-ups the Crown's efforts and expenses were not in vain.

Doodling a cartoon of Dow with a cock in his mouth, Gabe got up and tried the window again, slapping at the sash until his palms were red and hurting, telling the duty cop he couldn't think of anything else without air-conditioning, sliding the pad and pen under the door.

He didn't get hit that time, Gabe sitting on the bed, wondering again if the window was stuck or nailed shut, opened only the two inches.

The cop ignored him thumping at the casing and sash. Gabe pushing, prying, punching the sill with the heel of his hand, finally getting it unstuck.

A cool breeze pushed in past the dead heat. Swigging the Fanta the cop brought him, he looked down at the four-floor drop to the pavement, wondering what his chances were, surviving a jump like that. After he ate, the cop handed him the pad and pen back, along with a warning about drawing more filth. Told him if Gabe was a good boy, the cop would ask the owner about a fan.

Jotting some of the places he collected from, some of the names of the Junction crew, the lower-tier guys who worked the poker games with Lenny. Writing dates as best as he could remember, stuff he was pretty sure Dow already knew. Not going to give him any meat, just enough to wet the man's whistle — not till he had his deal in place. Once Dow had what he wanted, Gabe would be tossed off like a sack of trash.

Lying on the sagging mattress, he looked up at a roach crossing the ceiling, wondered how it did that with gravity working against it, watched it start down the far wall. Gabe thinking about how he'd drop like a rock out the window. He tomahawked his shoe at the roach, just ended up knocking the rabbit ears from the TV.

The cop asking, "What the hell you doing in there, Zoller?"

"Fucking with the bugs." Gabe looking at the darkening sky, turned the knob on the Zenith and dialed channel 6, then 9. The news showing Americans on a space walk, a fighter squadron off the USS *Midway* downing some North Vietnamese MiGs, McNamara sending more troops, an anti-war demonstration at the Pentagon.

Flicking between the channels, he got *Magistrate's Court*, followed by *Take 30*, then *This Hour Has Seven Days* — Gabe wanting to climb the walls. Switching again, putting up with a scratchy channel 11, getting a Lucy and Ricky rerun. Wondering what the redhead was like on her back, Gabe thinking he could be up for some rust lust.

The room cooled, but he spent a restless night. The sound of crickets and corn swaying in the light breeze. Next morning brought Commander Tom entertaining the kiddies, then some game show. By afternoon, he was back to Lucy, Gabe thinking about tying Ricky to a chair, how he'd get him babalu-ing along as Gabe did the little fire bunny. Didn't matter that the duty cop outside could hear. Leave a man locked in a room long enough, no guarantee what kind of witness Terrence Dow would be putting on the stand.

Continental breakfast was nearly the same as yesterday's: a Danish, a bottle of Sanka and an orange. Shutting off the set, letting the tubes cool, he sat in his underpants, pulling the chair to the open window, looking out at the road, thinking more and more about jumping to freedom. Lunch came disguised as tuna on white, along with a Pepsi and a limp celery stick.

The blond cop was back on duty, leading him down the hall for his constitutional, only chance of the day to stretch his legs. Gabe feeling how he was cramping up, guessing if he asked this guy about the fan, he'd just get punched in the gut again. Afternoon was solitaire with a deck the proprietor let him have, one of the kings had been torn and taped back together.

Tired of losing, he lay back on the bed, trading Lucy for Ginger and Mary Ann, thinking about a two-on-one on that three-hour tour. Supper came looking like it had been warmed from a can. Chili or stew, he couldn't tell.

Wondering if Terrence Dow got pulled from the case, or was off on some vacation, Gabe back to thinking about going out the window. When he went to the can, he flushed the toilet to muffle the sound, prying up the window as far as he could, trying to squeeze through the tiny bathroom window, but couldn't get his shoulders through.

The blond cop knocked on the door. "The fuck you doing in there, Zoller?"

Back in the room, Gabe considered jumping the cop, getting in a jab and following it with a solid hook, finish him and rush down to the ground floor and disappear through miles of corn. Gone by the time the cop figured what happened. North, south, west, it didn't matter. Gabe needed to get away from this Half Moon of hell. Sure Ernie Zimm had guys looking for him, knowing it was just a matter of time.

... *gunning for gabe*

L enny never saw it when they were dating or when they started talking about getting married. Paulina wanting to go with tradition, Lenny going along. Her friends-and-family ceremony turned out to be two hundred gathered to watch the couple under the chuppah, women with shoulders covered, men with yarmulkes. The seven blessings, the breaking glass, the Mitzvah tantz and all that good food.

Two years she'd been his sweet angel with that smile that could light up a room. The rift coming slow as the light faded. Paulina hating his secrets and late nights, followed by her headaches and not wanting to go out, blaming the downhill sex on the pain in her head. Lenny said he'd get the Aspirin, ended telling her she was being horrible. Paulina saying she wished she'd been horrible sooner. Well, she wanted out, then she was out. But Lenny wasn't giving up half of everything to a woman who was tired of having him around. Lenny betting she didn't get the headaches with the cop, Gary Evans.

The Portuguese messed it up, and Carlos paid the big price, Luís and Jaco charged with the robbery attempt. Pushing it out of his mind for now, he got back to why Dag Malek had called him at the Empress, said he wanted to see him, the two meeting at Fran's Restaurant late at night, Yonge and St. Clair. Dag taking a table in a corner. Their coffee coming, Dag pulling a flask and giving the cups a boost, started by saying, "That fucking Gabe."

"Yeah." Lenny looked around the place, picking up his cup, waiting for what was coming.

Dag not starting with one of his dumb jokes, getting straight to the point. "The man's got to go." He took a sip. "L'chaim."

"Yeah, l'chaim."

"Ernie wants you to do it."

Lenny sipped and stifled a cough. "I'm no hitter."

"The thing needs doing. Think of it like this, a chance to show what you can do, make a move up."

Like he needed to improve his résumé. Lenny taking his time, saying, "They got him in custody, right?" Shrugging like what could he do.

"Moved him to a secret spot." Dag reached the flask and topped Lenny's cup, then his own. "Keeping the rat safe."

"Gabe's a bit off center, but a rat ..." Lenny shaking his head. "He says anything to them, he's fucking with them, stringing them —"

"It's done, Lenny."

Lenny sipped some more.

"Take a guess, the first name he gave up. That's right, you, princess. Gave you up like that. Saving the rest of us for the main course."

Lenny sat there, trying to look surprised. He hated hearing it from Gary Evans. Gabe giving up his partner on the tenements, both on the hook to Ungerman. Not sure what the man had been thinking.

201

"Gabe's making a break tomorrow night."

"A break?" Lenny looked at him, knowing Zimm had people everyplace.

Dag took another sip. "He doesn't know it yet." Slinging an arm over the back of the chair, looking at him. "When he makes his move, you're gonna be there, pick him up."

Lenny waiting.

"Then you're gonna pop him."

Lenny set down his cup.

"Got him north of the city, a place called Goodwill. Keeping the rat safe till they can put him on the stand, pointing at you, me, Ernie, the whole outfit. Making it worth his while." Sipping again, Dag said, "Don't it make you mad?"

"Yeah, sure. I mean, if it's true."

"Came from the mick at the desk; a real piece of work, but you can take it to the bank. And speaking of the bank . . ." Dag reached in his jacket, took an envelope and slid it across. "Help you out with your own troubles."

Looking at the envelope, Lenny knowing they had guys for this kind of thing, over in the Junction, Syrian guys they could call up from Windsor or Detroit. Maybe Ernie found out about the buildings the two of them bought, his way of showing it pissed him off. Lenny saying, "Come on, Dag, you don't want me. Only thing I ever shot had *STOP* painted on it." Feeling the twist in his gut — could be they caught wind of him messing with the Portuguese, two of them in jail, the other one shot dead.

Felt he was starting to sweat in the shirt he grabbed back at the house, and the only clean one he had. Saw himself washing it in the sink tonight, the fucking room at the Empress. Hanging it on the shower rod, hoping it would dry by morning.

"You did okay that time with DiPalma," Dag said.

"That was all Gabe. I was ducking behind his fender. Fired across the hood, didn't even stick my head up."

"Yeah, but you were there, and you didn't run rabbit."

"Been thinking it coulda been me that plugged Gabe."

Dag laughed and said, "Yeah, we thought that too. Or, likely would've been two more dead wops. Think of it this way, you got in some batting practice, taking him out."

"Don't think you get what I'm saying?"

"That's what I like about you, Lenny, you don't blow your trumpet, you know? You keep it down low, straight up."

"Look, me and Gabe came up together, working the Ward, him doing his streets, me doing mine. Got some after-hour history, kinda chummy, you understand?"

"The kind of guy that can walk up to him, him not seeing it coming."

Lenny sat, no point arguing, thinking of that time — running into DiPalma and his crew, the two of them stumbling out of the Brunny, half-tanked on cheap draft, walking around the corner, going to Gabe's Catalina parked off Bloor. Laughing and bumping into each other — a shot coming from behind — Lenny jumping for the ground, and Gabe drawing his piece and going straight at them, shooting it out, Lenny ducking behind the Catalina, holding his .32 over the hood and firing. Gabe put DiPalma down, took a bullet in the side and kept firing, sending the other two running.

Gabe never said word-one about Lenny ducking behind his fender and shooting blind with Gabe in his line of fire, betting Gabe knew how he caught one in the side. The Catalina taking a round in the fender, one meant for Lenny.

"Why it's got to be you, Lenny, a guy he trusts. The one guy who can walk right up to him, a smile he can trust."

"Never gonna see the guy from Windsor coming either, just a stranger passing on the street, swinging in from behind. Over in a second. Me, I got to remember to take the safety off."

"You know why it's you, Lenny?" Dag said, starting to get impatient. "'Cause Ernie says it's you. You wanna tell him you're taking a pass, be my guest. He's a reasonable guy, you know that, right?"

Lenny drank the spiked coffee, felt it burn going down.

"You know, a guy in your spot, oughta have a better attitude." Dag sipped, saying, "Look Lenny, don't make too big a deal here. All you got to do is show up and take the safety off. The rat comes out a window and climbs down a bedsheet. You stick out your arm, say so long if you want. Do the deed and you drive off, toss the piece where I tell you. And we never speak about it again."

"He'll see it in my eyes."

"Too late by then." Dag nodded like he understood, then leaned across, resting his arms, trying one more time, saying, "I got you a clean piece and help you on the alibi. When it's done, we get you out of that firetrap you're living at. Put you up in style while you get your house in order." Showing Lenny that they knew everything going on. "Took it upon myself, got you booked in this place, a resort in Huntsville, right by the lake. Take a drive and clear your head. Got this dancer waiting to keep you company."

Lenny sat with it.

"Four hours north, right up the 11. You been there since last night, having the time of your life. Making up lost time since the wife tossed you out."

Lenny wanted to tell him he never cheated in his life, but Dag put up a hand, telling him how the Crown counsel moved Gabe to this dive hotel in a shoebox town, middle of no place. "Got him under protective custody. The cop guarding tomorrow night's going to the can same time Gabe goes out the window. You get the picture?"

Lenny looked out at St. Clair, like he was hoping there might be a way out.

Dag gave a thin smile, taking out the same snapshot Ross Cohen had shown Gabe. "She goes by Poppy. Not bad, am I right? Just don't go getting a heart attack on me."

Lenny looked at him.

"Your friend's a rat. Gave you up first." Dag looking at him for a reaction.

Lenny wondered how many guys Dag had clipped, talking like it was a walk in High Park, the man sitting at the right hand of Ernie Zimm. Manni Schiller on the other side. Telling people what to do and who they had to do it to.

Dag tapped a finger on the envelope, saying, "Help you with your Get."

How the hell did they know about that? Lenny just nodded.

"You say it like it's up to me, but the thing is, you're not really asking."

Dag shrugged, taking his flask and topping them again, saying, "You're a smart guy, Lenny. You see things like they are. Now come on, lighten up. You hear the one about Monty the pessimist talking to Izzy the optimist. Monty says, 'Things couldn't be any worse.' Izzy the optimist looks at him, says, 'Sure they could.'" Dag looking at Lenny, smiling, saying, "You get it?"

... *dame fortune*

"Well, you think about the rematch?" Gary Evans said as Paulina opened the door. Holding up a hand. "Please."

Looked like she was going to slam it back shut, then her shoulders softened, Paulina saying, "I thought I made —"

"A minute, okay?"

She stood holding the door, waiting, not asking him in, giving him that "the clock is ticking" look.

"Look, I got assigned this case —"

"Already said all that."

"It started out one way, then I got to know you . . ." Gary's look said indigestion. "And I got in deep, getting deeper by the minute, and I couldn't come out and say, 'By the way, I'm really out to bust your husband.'"

"Too honest?"

"Top of which I can't talk about an active case, but I can tell you . . ." He didn't know what to tell her.

Her look softened and she pulled the door back, saying, "You want coffee?"

Surprised. "If it's no trouble." He stepped in the marble foyer and looked around like something heavy might fall on him. Patting the poodle's head. Taking the shoes off, he followed her to the kitchen, looking at her from behind, the figure of an athlete, looking just as good in the stretch pants as she did in tennis whites. Pictured her in heels and one of those minis. Standing by the doorway, he watched her set up the percolator, still appraising, asking, "Anything I can do?"

"You've done plenty, Gary." Pointing him to a counter stool, saying, "So, what else you want off your chest?"

"Well, I know I'm on thin ice, but I got to ask, what got in your head, marrying a guy like Lenny?"

"Maybe I was young and dumb." She shrugged. "I don't know, maybe he was from the tribe, good-looking enough and he had prospects."

"You ever believe he sold cruises?"

"What it says on his tax return." She smiled, then shrugged. "No, I knew who he was."

"Then why?"

The coffee was dripping, Paulina shrugged, leaning across from him and said, "You think I'm in on it, with the mob?" She made a finger gun.

"No, see you as more of a victim."

"Still want to squeeze me for information?"

"I guess he never told you much. Still, I want to believe you'd do the right thing. And yeah, some squeezing crossed my mind." Felt himself blush as he smiled.

"While seizing my assets?"

"If you do help out, there'll be leniency. And maybe you get a warm feeling, doing the right thing."

"You bag Lenny, you get a promotion, right?"

"I'm not out to hurt you, Paulina."

The two of them looked at each other, the coffee perking and dripping in the pot. Then she leaned forward, cupped a hand around his neck and kissed him on the mouth. Drawing back, meeting his eyes, saying, "How do you take it?"

"Later." Gary caught his breath, reached and kissed her again, held it this time. "One more thing . . ."

"Yeah?"

"Really think you can beat me — straight sets?"

"Whip you like a dog."

He smiled, tried to pull her close, and she pushed from him and started up the stairs.

"Guess we're heading for that rematch." And he followed.

. . . going for zoller

T he Galaxie bounded over a pothole, the springs no
match for the bounce, the undercarriage bottoming out.
Lenny's head tapping the headliner, gravel pinging off the
chrome and Caspian-blue paint. Driving north of the city,
the evening sky filling with stars, dusk giving up the ghost.
Lenny keeping to the middle of the two-lane, easing it to
thirty when the gravel became dirt, the suburbs becoming
the outskirts, barns and farmhouses, dark bovine shapes in
open fields. The dirt road narrowed to a single lane, ditches
on either side, deep as moats, tall grass hiding the drop, corn
in the fields behind it.

Driving till he saw the lighted sign, showing from a
quarter mile off, the place called the Half Moon. Lenny
played it through his mind: how Dag told him to get his
mind right and do it quick. Reminded him that Gabe gave
him up first. Dag handing him the ugly .38-cal Smith after
they left Fran's, a throwaway piece with its serials filed away.
Maybe it had killed before. It jostled under the car seat when
he hit another pothole.

Dag called it that, a throwaway — like killing Gabe meant nothing. Drawing him a map on a napkin, Dag explaining where to drop the piece after — a farm lake out past Bolton. Behind a big barn that doubled as a weekend dancehall for the locals. Step on a wooden dock and chuck it far into the murk, the silt bottom taking care of the rest. Then he was to drive north, get on the 11, Poppy the go-go dancer waiting in Huntsville, swearing he'd been there since yesterday.

Lenny kept his own troubles from nudging into his mind. Gabe Zoller had to go, and if he messed this up, he'd likely end up in the unmarked hole next to Gabe.

The watch Paulina gave him told him he was making good time, dusk settling as he pulled to the gravel shoulder, a hundred yards south of the motel, Lenny careful not to drop a wheel off the soft shoulder. Turning off the engine to the sound of crickets. Looking at the hotel sign and its tin roof, reaching across and rolling down the passenger and rear windows, letting air flow through the interior. The corn hissing a concerto with the crickets.

A simple set-up is what Dag called it, easy as pie. The cop on duty was bringing Gabe extra bedding. Dag trusting Gabe had enough smarts to see his chance to escape: tie the sheets together and climb out the window he'd been banging on since he got there — the cop going downstairs to turn up the radio and play checkers with the proprietor.

Lenny waiting for Gabe to come ass-first out the window, shimmying down the bedsheets. Soon as his feet touched the dirt, Lenny would be there, putting the ugly .38 on him, get him in the car and drive west on 7A. Stop in the middle of no place, stand Gabe at the ditch and put one in his brainpan, leave him where he fell. Follow the map Dag sketched, find the farm lake and fling the piece off the dock. Then drive north to Huntsville, let Poppy and a bottle take his mind off it.

The engine cooled, the metal pinging. Pulling his legs up and across the seat, careful his knees didn't bang the horn. Dusk slipping into evening, the cricket ensemble going to full symphony, playing to the stars.

Stepping out, he arched his back, remembered watching Paulina working out in the tights, along to Jack LaLanne on the TV, the man showing how to do it, wearing the same tights that didn't look right on a man. Lenny pictured himself knocking on her door and showing her the ugly .38, saying something like, "You want a Get, here it is. Mazel tov, baby." Give her a chance to come up with a line — the woman always needing to get in the last word. Giving him a look that said he couldn't do it. Folding her arms, going all princess and telling him to beat it.

Lenny pulled the trigger in his mind. Yeah, he could do it.

Knowing his sweet angel was planning to take the cop upstairs when he showed with the bag of deli. The cop with his wife, cuffing her wrists to the frame of the sacred marriage bed, the bedroom set Lenny still owed three payments on. Screwing his wife, Paulina feeding him information like grapes, fucking Lenny over twice. Yeah, he could do it. Knock on her door, wait till it opened, and pull the trigger.

And like that, an idea came to him, a better way to do it. Lenny playing with it, looking at it from all angles, finally eyeing his watch — Gabe was supposed to come out the upstairs window, Lenny lifting his hands from the wheel of the Galaxie. They were clammy, but not shaking. And he was ready.

... *pillow talk*

"That was something." Gary turned his head to Paulina, smiling and clicking his teeth. "Love that thing you do ..."

"Did, not do. Now *shh*."

"Like a little lick ..."

"If I wanted Walter Cronkite telling me the way it is, I'd've called him over."

"Don't like talking after, huh?"

"Not really into a 'was it good for you' chat." Paulina thinking they should have gone to a hotel — having sex in this bed feeling wrong. Baby lying by the door, the dog giving her a look, making her feel guilty.

"Okay, I get it."

"Look, we didn't plan it, it just happened. Probably the only time it will. But talking about it takes something away ..."

"Like the magic?"

"You're a nut." But she was smiling. Definitely should have gone to a hotel.

"Well, you ask me, it's the start of something." Gary looked over the side, reaching his Jockeys.

"It was sex, Gary. Let's not dissect it."

"Right." He sat up, zipped his lip, looking at the floor for his scattered clothes.

"We played singles, you wanting to nail my ex. In the end you got both of us. Works out for you. So let's leave it at that." She sat up, surprised at herself, hostility not usually following sex. Standing naked, she felt him looking at her, she got her robe around herself, saying the coffee was getting bitter. Wondering why she was feeling a mix of guilt and hostility. Telling herself to let it go.

"Sure." Gary tugged on a sock, looking around for his other one.

Finding it in the sleeve of the robe, she held it on her finger, letting go a sigh, saying, "Here you go."

"I want to see you, get to know you." Gary taking the sock.

She opened her robe, then dropped it to the carpet, took the sock from him and tossed it, saying, "Coffee's stale anyhow. So get to know me some more."

. . . *busting out*

"Your lucky day, Zoller. You get clean sheets." The blond cop with the sour look held out the folded sheets and pillow case.

"You boys doubling as room service, huh?" Gabe guessed a punch was coming, this time ready for it, set to knock this jerk on his ass.

The cop dropped the bedding to the floor, swept it in with his foot, saying, "Housekeeper's day off, so you get to do it yourself, you want those nice hotel corners."

This cop had the same attitude as the rest Dow had sent here, not the serve-and-protect kind. Shutting the door. Gabe hearing the key turn in the lock, the cop settling on the creaking chair outside.

Picking up the bedding, an idea came to him, how to get out of there. Don Messer ending, Gabe switching channels, catching the opening credits for *Gunsmoke* coming on. By the time *For the People* started, Gabe had it clear in his mind.

After the fricassee supper, the balding hotel owner collected the dishes, asked Gabe how it was.

"It was something alright."

Then he had the cop escort him to the can. On the way back, the cop told him Terrence Dow was coming in the morning, had some news for him, didn't think from Dow's reaction it was good news, but didn't know more than that. Gabe complained his stomach was flipping from that chicken fuck-assee, saying, "Ought to look and see if there's a pigeon missing off the roof."

"Naw, that was roadkill," the cop said. "Pretty squished to tell what it was, groundhog's my guess."

"Thanks. So, unless you're gonna tuck me in —"

The cop shoved him back to the bed and said, "Nighty night." And swung the door shut.

Switching off the lights, Gabe waited, then he worked by the light of the TV, keeping the volume low, tying the bedsheets corner to corner, getting a tight knot. Betty Grable and Trini Lopez on *The Tonight Show* when he figured the time was right, hearing the cop clomp down the stairs. Fastening one end to the radiator, unfurling the rest like a rope out the window. The sheets didn't make it all the way down, but it had to be close enough.

Putting a foot on the ledge, he went out off the sill, trying to be quiet, lowering and climbing down the bedding hand over hand like Tarzan, clinging onto the sheet. He lowered himself down, careful not to bang against the siding. Got halfway when he felt the sheet above tear, dropping him a foot. And he clung to it, still two stories up. The sheet ripped more, Gabe not yelling as he fell.

Landing on his back with a thump. Dust rising into his nostrils. The wind knocked from his lungs. Staring up until he could move again, hearing the goddamn corn in the field, the sound of the husks and crickets, stars above in the ink of night. The cop didn't show at the upper window he'd climbed from.

Forcing his legs under him, he put his hand to the ground and yelped. The pain like a knife. And he tucked the arm close, looking around as he rose. Holding his arm to his body, he looked for a car in the empty lot. Not seeing one, he started for the wall of corn across the road. He would push through the stalks, disappear and tend to the arm later.

Nearly to the asphalt when an engine jumped on, a car's shape rolling from the south, just past the hotel property, its headlights off. Freezing for a moment, he hobbled for the opposite ditch, set to pitch himself into the corn as the car slowed, the driver's voice low and coming from the open window, "How's the action here, brother?"

Lenny sat behind the wheel, grinning at him, hanging an arm out the window.

Didn't move right away, then Gabe went around the hood, his good hand flat on it like Lenny might try to run him over, and he got in the passenger side, looking over the back seat and down on the rear floor.

"Glad to see me, huh?" Lenny drove off easy.

Gabe saw the pistol in Lenny's left hand, across his lap, pointing at him. "You, huh, Lenny?"

"Hear you been talking me up to your new friends."

"They got you believing I'm a rat."

"That, or maybe it's your lucky day." Lenny smiled.

"I'm having trouble seeing it."

"Dag promised me a dancer on a pole, waiting for me in Huntsville."

"Same one they promised me. Poppy, right?"

"That's her." Lenny nodded.

"The cop in on it?" Gabe said.

"Believe there'll be something extra in his pay."

Gabe looked at the pistol, Lenny holding it across his body, steering with his right.

"So, on top of the go-go chick, they paying you enough?" Gabe said.

"You mean on account of my conscience . . . yeah, not too bad. They figure you'd see me, and it'd put you at ease, get you in the car."

"Except you never done it in your life. Like the time you ducked behind my fender . . . and I know it was you shot me."

"Yeah, it's been weighing on me." Lenny guessing Gabe wouldn't believe he just shot Carlos, left him dead with the futebol playing.

"Not how it's looking."

"Tried to tell Dag I was wrong for it, this kind of thing. But, Ernie, you know how he gets, the man wants it done, and Dag's talking like it's some big step up. You know what I think, they got wind of you and me buying the buildings."

"So you gonna fix them up on your own, owing Ungerman the whole nut."

"Just got some extra cash . . . plus the girl on the pole."

"And you can live with that?"

"I don't know yet." Still aiming the pistol across his body, driving steady, Lenny smiled, saying, "Remember that glass-eyed gal at the Elmo, the one turned you down flat?"

Gabe nodded, saying, "Except it was Le Coq d'Or, but yeah, sure, I remember. Lots of 'em turned me flat, all up and down the Strip."

"What did you call them two, kitty punchers? Oh, man —" Lenny laughed and shook his head.

"That where we're going, down memory lane. Gonna get me soft, then pop me?"

Lenny looked at the pistol in his hand, then at Gabe holding the arm, then back at the dark road. "It busted?"

"Feels like it, yeah."

No streetlights out in the sticks. Lenny saying, "One thing I got to know, drinking pals aside —"

"I'm no rat."

"Not what I'm asking. Want to know if it was you, and Ernie told you to do it . . ."

"What, shoot myself?"

"Shoot me. If it was me who screwed the pooch as bad as you."

"Wouldn't do it. No way."

"Yeah, you would."

"But this is you we're talking about, and Lenny, you're no hitter. Just like I'm no rat."

"Dag said you gave me up first."

Gabe let some time pass, then said, "It matter what I tell you?"

"Not so much, no."

"So how you gonna do it, pull to the side, get me to step out, or do it right on your fake leather?"

"You in a rush?"

"Let's say I got an interest."

"You fucked up, Gabe. Don't go woe-is-me, okay?"

"I was having a rough day, sure. That fucking building you talked me into. Being in hock to Ungerman . . ."

"There's your trouble, man, you take no responsibility, and you got no vision." Lenny slid the pistol under the seat, taking the wheel in both hands, saying, "As far as kiboshing your sorry ass, I got a better way . . ."

Gabe looked at him, now hopeful, saying, "Yeah . . . well, I'd sure like to hear about it."

"We had some good times, right, you and me?"

"Sure we did."

"You thinking you're good with the ladies."

"You want me fixing you up, just say the word."

"Never had a problem fixing myself up. Trouble started when I broke the glass."

"Maybe you better spell it out."

A mile from the hotel now, Lenny pulled to the gravel and stopped the car, somewhere around where he was supposed to pop Gabe, and he left the engine idling. "What I'm saying, maybe we can help each other out."

"I'm all ears." Gabe easing, seeing Lenny wasn't going to shoot him. No need to dive for the pistol with one arm busted.

"Having trouble on the home front, maybe you heard."

"What, the nice blonde?"

"Yeah, the missus."

"And a good-looking one too, you don't mind me saying."

"Yeah, a lot of good it did me."

"You want me talking to her, set her straight?"

Lenny reached over and put his hand on Gabe's broken arm.

Gabe biting his teeth together, wincing as he growled through the pain.

"Want her straightened out . . . for a pine box. But, first we got to get your arm wrapped up."

"Can't walk in no Mount Sinai . . ."

"Gonna let the swelling go down, then get it splinted and wrapped."

"You playing doctor?"

"Call it another first."

Gabe frowned, saying, "So, this woman trouble . . ."

"The wife wants a Get . . . on account she's seeing this cop."

"She's schtupping a cop?"

"Yeah, one trying to nail the outfit, you believe that?"

"So if I'm not talking to her, then what, slapping some sense . . ."

"I want to call up my insurance man, talk about the life policies her and me took when we got hitched. Case one of us got cancer, hit by a car, or something."

"You want me taking care of the something?"

Lenny put it in gear and kept driving, letting him think about it as he headed west on the rural road, then south on a two-lane, heading back toward the city lights. One thing was sure, this had to go right, or he'd end up just as dead as Gabe was going to be.

. . . the canary can sing, but he can't fly

"Well, find the fuck out." Ernie slammed down the phone.

Dag Malek stepped in with a pair of take-out cups, swallowing the joke he was set to tell — a good one about an anti-Semite going in the bar, sees a Jew in a kippah and orders a round for everybody but the Jew. The Jew smiling and thanking the guy, the anti-Semite ordering a second round, again the Jew smiles and thanks him. The hater asking the bartender, "What the fuck's wrong with that guy?" Being told the Jew owns the place — Dag deciding to hold back the Shecky Greene routine, instead saying, "Called Lenny's place, but the wife hangs up on me." Sitting down opposite, sliding one of the coffees across the desk, taking the lid off his own and blowing across the top — man, he wanted to tell the joke.

Ernie looking at him deadpan, saying, "What?"

"Manni's gone to talk some sense to her, but you ask me, Lenny's got a domestic beef of atomic proportions."

"Fuck his beef. I want to know what he did with that rat-fuck. Goddamn, I asked the man a simple thing — wait under a window and pop the guy. That asking too much?"

221

"The cop said no shots got fired, at least not there." Dag shifted in his chair, trying his coffee, saying, "Said Gabe had the sheets out the window. Ripped partway down, looked like he took a tumble. But, no sign of him or Lenny."

"So the rat runs through the corn, and Lenny's a no-show, a guy with better things to do. Maybe the two of them driving up to Huntsville, taking turns with the chick on the pole, the one I paid for."

"We got people looking. Eyes on their places, train station, the airport, the whole town. Cops got Gabe's wheels in impound and an all-points on Lenny's ride. Where they gonna go?"

"How about hospitals, clinics, like that?"

Dag nodded, saying, "Even checked the vets."

"So, Lenny helps him get away, the two of them out there, and meantime you're sitting there drinking coffee, trying to figure how to tell me a joke." Ernie stared at him.

"I mean, if you want to hear one, sure, I got . . ."

Ernie dialed up the stare.

Getting up, Dag took his cup and thought of something he had to do.

. . . some woman

Manni Schiller knocked and stood back on the stoop, could hear music playing from inside, "Girl from Ipanema." Looking at the place, a trellis with ivy, a brick two-story with a double-car garage, trim lawn with a flower garden, trees like a canopy up and down the shaded street, thinking Lenny was doing alright for himself, wondering what the hell was going on with him.

Just had to drive up to the Half Moon, the place the prosecutor was hiding the rat and do a little exterminating. Didn't matter that Manni knew Gabe for better than a decade, even had him to the house a time or two. A rat was a rat and business was business. And Gabe knew the rules.

And Lenny was cashing an extra five large, help him with the upkeep of this nice-looking place, the kind of place couples moved to raise kids. But who knew, maybe Lenny had trouble pulling the trigger, even after Dag explained it to him.

The door opened, the music louder, and there she stood, bright eyes going cold as she recognized him, saying, "Already said he's not here."

Smiling at this wife of Lenny's, met her once before at a local ball game, the community team Ernie Zimm put money behind, bought the kids' uniforms and equipment. Good-looking and not hiding all that blonde hair under some wig, Manni remembered her as smart too. Meaning Lenny was a lucky guy.

"How you doing, Paulina. I'm Manni. Maybe you remember from the ball game. I was selling the franks, warming the buns. Good seeing you again."

She stood and looked at him, waiting.

"So, any idea where he is?"

"You the one who called?"

"That would be Dag. He's looking too."

"Well, you're in the wrong place."

"Sure you got no idea?"

"Very — and I don't want to know." She started to shut the door.

Manni put out a hand, kept it from closing. Looked sorry for doing it, saying, "Look, Paulina, it were up to me, I'd take your word, but I go back to Ernie and tell him I asked but didn't have a look around . . ."

"You think you're coming in and searching my house?" Her eyes sparkled, like they dared him to try it.

"If you don't mind . . ." Manni kept the hand on the door, seeing a pair of men's loafers on the tile floor, guessing Lenny was hiding inside. Smiling at her.

"I could call a cop." She gave a tight smile back, then seeing there was no point pushing back on the door, she let it go.

"Yeah, you could, but I'm still coming in. Be long gone before they get here. Besides, we're all friends here." He pushed past her, standing in the hall, looking around, a nice vase of white flowers on the hall table, a woman's touch. Music playing from the front room, a white poodle looking from the top of the stairs, trimmed up like a hedge, a ball of fur on its tail. Didn't look the guard-dog type. Manni commented on the music, saying, "That like a rhumba or something?"

"Bossa nova."

"That right, huh? Yeah, got a catchy beat." Like he gave a shit, he made a fox trot move, then said, "Really am sorry to push in, Paulina, but how about you play nice, tell Lenny to come on down; him and I got to talk. Maybe you go fix us a pot of joe."

"Like I'm the maid?"

"Like you're being friendly."

The song ended in the living room, the sound of the record scraping, then the needle being lifted, the single being changed, the tone arm touching down and a Beatles hit coming on.

Manni smiled, taking a step toward the living room, guessing Lenny was in there.

Paulina left the door hanging open, picked up the vase, hefted it behind him like she might crown him with it.

Manni caught the movement and took it from her, some water sloshing on his jacket. Standing and holding it in both hands when he saw the man sitting down in the easy chair near the living room window, not Lenny, but some guy looking his way — the cop who walked into the travel agency on Tuesday afternoon.

"Well, well . . ." Is all Manni could say, setting the vase back down.

"He's the cop I'm going to call," Paulina said, straightening the vase on the table.

Manni faced Gary Evans, saying, "Looks like an angel, but she's all spitfire, am I right?"

Gary just kept looking at him.

Manni saying, "Now, let's see if I got this —"

Gary got up slow and walked toward him, saying, "How about you just get to why you came."

"You wanna show me the shield again, the one that lets you tell me how it is, or maybe we gonna dance this time?" Manni moving enough to show the piece under his own jacket.

"Can show it to you, then I'm going to ask to see the registration for what's under the jacket."

"And what, take me in for wanting coffee?"

"Want you going back and telling your boss Lenny's not here. Like the lady said, she's got no idea where he is."

"You know he won't like it."

"Whatever Lenny's into, she doesn't know. He's out of her life. Looks like he's out of Ernie's life too. And far as what your boss thinks, I don't give a shit."

Manni said he'd let Ernie know, then stepped for the door.

"Oh, and Manni?" Paulina moved for the door, holding it open.

He turned on the welcome mat.

"You come back, I'll shoot you myself." Paulina gave him a sweet smile and waited till he walked down the steps.

"No doubt about it, sweetie," he said. Manni went along the walkway, putting it together, the cop in her living room, with his shoes off, listening to music. Manni believing Lenny wasn't coming back. Getting in his car, he remembered a piece in the *National Geographic*, one about bronco riders in Calgary trying to stay on top. Worth the thrill that lasted no more than seconds, getting on top of something like that, risking life and limb before getting pitched to the ground. Thinking of Paulina Ovitz like that.

... *doing the wife*

L enny wound the tensor wrap around the makeshift splint on the forearm, as tight as Gabe's moaning allowed, the paint stick from the Decorate Your World next door to the Rexall Drugs, the hilltop mall out by Bolton. Lenny put in the pins and looked at his handiwork, saying, "There we go."

"We, huh?" Speaking through gritted teeth, Gabe opened his eyes, looking at the sling rigged from the torn strip of drop cloth. "So when you want this done?"

"Doing the wife, let's call it that."

"You two try seeing the rabbi, therapy, all that?"

"Going Dear Abby again?"

"Was there when you did the mitzvah dance, and I don't know, maybe it's still got a chance ..."

"Sentimental for a guy who popped the Greek, then put one in back of his gal's wig."

"And maybe I got regrets."

"You gonna do it or not?"

"Just don't want it dogging you."

"Don't worry about me."

"How you gonna sell it to Ernie, me not ending in a ditch?"

"You got a manhunt on your ass, worry about that."

"And I hate bringing it up, but there's the buildings. Any money I had . . ."

Lenny reached and took what he had in the wallet and held it out. "Get you more when I can."

Doing a rough count, Gabe nodded and tucked it away, about two hundred bucks.

Lenny reached under the seat, took the ugly .38 and handed it to him grip first.

"Like it to go quick, or you want her to see it coming?" Gabe pulled the clip, checking the load.

Lenny saying, "I ain't no animal."

Gabe nodded and tucked the piece in his belt.

. . . *fathers and daughters*

"It's been over a while, Poppa." She'd glossed over the ledger pages, double-checking entries, betting he'd seen it as the biggest mistake of her life and known it all along. Coming to work, not wanting to be in the house alone — thinking Ernie Zimm's man could be parked across from the tiny park, staking out the house, waiting till Gary was gone. Maybe he followed her here, keeping a watch for Lenny.

It wasn't her regular day to be in the shop, but she didn't want her poppa on his own either, knowing he wouldn't back down from a guy like Manni Schiller. Seeing him getting older, thinner and grayer these days. And she wanted to be straight up about her split and tell him about Gary too, the parts he hadn't already figured out.

"I'm sorry, ketsele?" Isaac glanced up from his case, organizing the fall line.

She knew he'd seen her pain, betting he was going to say something like "it's for the best."

Instead, he said, "Lenny's not all bad —"

"We heading for a lecture, Poppa?"

"You'll know what to do, Schatz."

"I wish it was true."

"What we get for raising a strong girl, and smart like her mother." His wife Helen gone two years, leukemia taking her at sixty-six, about a million years too soon. Isaac saying after the service how he wished it had been him instead. The only time Paulina had seen him weep.

Now, it was just father and daughter. Long past saving his little girl from scraped knees, but he was still the poppa, and he'd always be there. Never saying anything against Lenny, but she knew how he felt since the first time she brought him around, Poppa pegging him for a knacker, the kind who ought to sell aluminum siding from behind that smile of his. Had his baby girl believing his gangster lies, at least for a while. Funny, she didn't see it from the start. And Poppa knew who Ernie Zimm was. Lenny going out the door every morning like he was peddling cruises to Miami, doing his shady deals — a shallow man in a deep pool.

"You come and stay at the house," Poppa said.

"And who's going to dust my place?"

"Was hoping you'd dust mine."

"Anytime you want." She smiled. "But, I'm fine, Poppa. Really."

"And if he comes back?"

"Lenny never dusted in his life."

"Don't joke."

"If he shows up, he better have the Get. He gives me any trouble, I call the cops."

And he smiled.

"Don't play with me, Poppa."

"You tell your heart to take its time."

"You're jumping ahead, way ahead." Rolling her eyes, then smiling, her poppa watching out for his little girl. "But he causes any trouble, how about I call you?"

"You can take care of yourself, ketsele, I know that, but it's good to be the poppa."

This man who survived the nightmare of the camps, stood holding the Maschendraht, dirty and starving in the striped rags, but hanging on to life when the allies rolled up in their Willys jeeps. It gave her comfort having him there, plus she had Gary the cop, and the two-shot derringer in her bag. Saying, "You worry if you have to, but just a little, okay?"

He clapped his hands to show he was moving on. Asking what she thought of the new Jaeger line, looking at his display.

"Think I like the Breitling, the one with the black dial." Guessing she knew why he asked, her birthday only a month away.

"Good taste like your mother." Isaac laid the black watch in the center of the raised display, trusting her judgement. When he closed the glass top, he said, "Now, how about we get a bite?"

"It's Friday, Poppa." Meaning the local haunts were closed for Shabbat, even Mica's.

"I was thinking Italian."

She raised a brow.

"Nice little place on Eglinton, all homemade."

"But not kosher?"

"But close enough."

"Guess I'd like that, except . . . I have a date."

"Your cop?"

"How about a raincheck?

"He observe the Shabbat?"

Her poppa asking if he was from the tribe, Paulina saying, "Why not come with, and you can ask him yourself?"

"What, go on your date?"

"You can tell me what you think after."

"What am I, a third wheel?"

"Come on, Poppa, it'll be fun." Paulina smiled, imagining the look on Gary's face, bringing her poppa on a date. Looking him over with those poppa eyes, give Gary a taste of what it's like being interrogated.

. . . death do us part

Isaac Levine knew who the man was as soon as he saw him. Already through the outer door, too late to step behind the mantrap door, he put an arm out and kept Paulina back. This gangster from his past, back when his shop was on Augusta, down in the Ward, all those years ago — this shakedown man working for Ernie Zimm. He came that time to tell him it was a hundred the beginning of every month, the cost of doing business. Wanted the first payment on the spot. Isaac had looked at him and put a hand under his counter, told him he should consider what a man might be holding in his hand before coming around asking for money. The gangster grinned like he figured Isaac was bluffing. Isaac saying he was free to find out and held the man's gaze. It was the customer coming in that had the shakedown man thinking better of it, telling Isaac he'd be back. Isaac said if he did come back, he best not start with hello.

When Isaac closed the shop that night, he went straight to Ernie Zimm's travel agency, a few blocks away at the time, walked past the clowns at the sales desks and into the man's office, didn't bother to knock. Told Ernie, "You send your man again, get ready to sit shiva, then see how many trips you're going to sell." Isaac who knew the rabbis, the assembly at synagogue, many of the shop owners in the Market, chummy with Lastman, Yuchtman, Phillips the former mayor, and was a paid member in high standing at the Primrose Club. Rapping his knuckles on Ernie's desk, not afraid to hold the gangster's eyes, then turning and stopping by the door, saying, "And, Ernie, ask around, I know a lot of Jews." With that he left, thinking it was the end of it.

Now this shakedown man was back, standing in front of his place, his left arm in a sling. Isaac kept Paulina behind him.

"Yeah, you remember me, old man."

Isaac stared and waited.

... *two birds, one stone*

G abe Zoller drew the .38. The old man pushing Lenny's ex behind him. Gabe seeing he'd have to do them both. This old man who had it coming from that long time ago. Refusing to pay, and Gabe catching shit from Ernie, in the end being told to lay off the jeweler. Asking him now, "Remember what you said that time, old man?"

"The money's in the drawer," Isaac said, held up his keys and half-turned to the door like he wanted to get back inside. Kept a hand on Paulina's arm.

"I'll get it after." Gabe cocked the pistol, wagging it at him, saying, "You walked into Zimm's, told Ernie if I come back be ready to sit shiva." He smiled, then said, "Now move aside, let's have a look at the tokhter. Girl all grown up." Gabe wanting the old man to see her go first.

Isaac didn't move.

"You don't get a say this time, old man." Gabe lowered the barrel to Isaac's knee. "Don't move, it's gonna hurt like hell, then it'll end the same way."

Isaac stared at Gabe like he was ready.

"Didn't think so." Stepping closer, Gabe had another quick look around.

Outside, with no chance of getting behind the shatterproof doors, Isaac lunged and grabbed at the pistol, tried to deflect it as it went off.

Deafened, Paulina was knocked back, catching her poppa from falling. Blood across the side of his head, his mouth open like he couldn't believe it. Knees going out from under him, Paulina easing him to the ground.

The man stood over them, glancing around quickly, putting the pistol on her. "Was you I come to see, sweet thing."

She looked up through the tears, Gabe seeing the derringer coming out of her bag, then a shot punched him forward. Staying on his feet, he tried to raise his arm, his feet tangling and he staggered, looked confused as the pistol fell from his grip; and he keeled forward and was down on the pavement, on his knees.

Gabe tried to focus, tried to make his fingers work, reaching for the pistol on the ground. He'd been shot from behind, not by the wife. He turned his neck enough, looking up at Lenny standing over him, his .32 in his hand. Second time he'd been shot by the same gun. Through the pain, Gabe tried to put it together. Lenny sent to kill him, instead handing him the murder weapon, setting him up for ... what? He turned back to the blonde, the woman bent over the old man and crying, blood on her hands. He croaked to her, "It was Lenny."

She turned, her eyes dripping tears.

And Lenny shot him again, flattening him to the pavement. Gabe felt the punch of it, but not the pain this time. The blood staining the sidewalk, wondering if it was his or the old man's. And he started to drift.

. . . too far from shore

L enny slid the .38 away with his foot, looking at Gabe
and seeing it was done. Putting away his own pistol, he
stepped past the body. Gabe had been a dead man either way,
but in the end Lenny couldn't let him shoot her, something
he had to do himself. Now, he was looking at her, reaching
a hand to her arm, realizing it looked like he rescued her.

She was kneeling over Isaac, crying and telling him to
hang on.

Lenny went past her, but couldn't get in the doors,
needing to call an ambulance.

Paulina clawed her keys from her bag, handing them to
him. Lenny working the colored keys in the locks, went to the
phone behind the glass display, dialing the emergency number
361-1111. Telling dispatch shots had been fired, two men and a
woman were down outside Isaac's Jewelers. Remembered the
address. And he hung up.

Using the keys, going back out, he told Paulina the medics
were on the way, checking that no one else was around.

Paulina glanced up through the tears. "He said it was you."

"Guess he meant I shot him." Lenny looking down at the old man, his blood on the sidewalk. Looked like Gabe's bullet caught the side of his head — counting on the reaper beating the ambulance. Didn't matter this old man was tough as gristle. A camp full of Nazis couldn't kill him, leaving it up to Lenny Ovitz twenty years later.

Turning, he nudged Gabe in the ribs with the toe of his shoe. Making sure. The guy he stood with against the Italians, the guy who was his partner, guy who ratted him out.

"You put him up to it," she said.

"Why don't you ask him?" And they were back at it, arguing, Lenny looking at the .38 on the ground. "I come by, hand you your Get, and end up saving your life. And what do I get?" And he was looking at Gary Evans's reflection in the jewelry store glass, walking up and standing there with flowers. The guy looking dumbfounded, in a nice sport jacket and tie. Lenny grinned at him, putting his pistol on him.

... scene of the crime

Gary Evans had his AM playing in the car, thought he heard a gunshot over the Otis Redding number, deciding it was a car backfiring. Parking in the lot, he got out and started for the jeweler's, seeing them out front. Two men on the ground, Paulina was kneeling and crying, Lenny Ovitz standing over the other one, toeing him, bending for a pistol on the ground. Reaching under his own jacket, realizing he hadn't come armed, Gary coming to take Paulina to see *Cat Ballou*, Lee Marvin supposed to be something to behold. A quiet dinner after, then see where it went from there. Gary hoping they might pick up where they left off. Maybe check into a hotel this time. Now, he was saying to Lenny, "Let me see some hands."

Lenny looked up at him holding a bunch of flowers, the cop he traded punches with, the one screwing his wife. Smiling, Lenny aimed at him, "What'd I tell you about dating my wife?"

"Ex-wife." Paulina looked up from her poppa. "You brought it, right, Lenny — the Get?" Getting him to look her way.

"Man, once you start, you don't quit."
And she held out her arm and shot him.

. . . *fade out*

Felt like a punch, and he was staggering, his world was tipping, his head hitting the sidewalk. And he lay there, turning his neck to look at her, then trying to speak, having trouble breathing. Then he was looking into the eyes of the old man, staring back at him. Both of them on the sidewalk. A thin smile on the old man's lips. And Lenny tried with everything he had left, to move his arm along the ground, just to shoot the old man. Saw the wedding band still on his own finger.

A shoe came into his vision, sweeping the pistol past his reach. Lenny turned enough to see her and the cop up above him. The sirens in his ears, his eyes tilting to the old man on the sidewalk — sure the old man was grinning at him — the night sky above the sign: Isaac's Jewelers, since 1946.

$$\ldots c_{17}h_{19}no_3$$

S he took her poppa's hand, telling him he'd be alright. He had to be alright.

Isaac looked at her from the gurney, the attendants moving him and sliding him in back of the ambulance. Giving her a smile, squeezing her hand, saying, "Of course, I'm alright." His voice weak, trying to sound sure.

When he woke again, it was daylight, and he was in a hospital room — her hand still holding his — a smell about the place, like disinfectant masking sickness. A nurse in white was moving from the room, a beeping monitor next to the bed. And he tried to remember through the painkiller's fog. Focusing on Paulina, trying to smile. He swallowed, his throat coated in sand, tongue like cloth, and he got the words out. "You look awful, ketsele."

He looked up at the drip in the line, following the tube down, the line taped to his forearm. Trying to make sense.

"You were shot, Poppa."

He tried to remember, and some of the pieces came together: a man putting a gun on him as he grabbed for it. He smiled at her, saying, "It was nothing."

Paulina guessed the painkillers were at full volume.

"That man with the gun . . ." Isaac said, frowning like he wasn't sure if he dreamed it.

"Lenny shot him."

Isaac frowned, trying to understand, looking around, saying, "He here? I should thank him."

"I'll explain later, Poppa." Paulina saying it like even the drip wouldn't stop him. He wanted answers, but right then all he could do was hold her hand.

Then the cop was stepping in the room. Gary Evans standing next to her, taking her free hand, looking down at him.

"He arrest you?" Isaac said.

"No, Poppa." And she smiled at Gary, repeated what the doctor had told her about her poppa's condition, calling it stable. Saying he was going to pull through.

Gary saying he was happy to hear it.

As drugged as he was, Isaac said, "So it was Lenny?"

And she nodded.

Isaac looked at Gary, not bad-looking for a goy cop. "You take care of her." Isaac trying for the "or else" look.

"I will, sir."

"No more talk now, Poppa. You need your rest. Sleep now." She leaned and kissed his forehead. Said she was glad the fever broke.

"What fever?" His voice a croak, and he was drifting again, his head feeling light and his body heavy, more tired than he'd ever been.

⸻

And then he was standing at a workbench, the early sun coming through the window, back at a time when he was a young apprentice, strong of body and curious of mind, intrigued by the tiny works that made the time tick. The tiny wheels and pivots, regulator and balance cock. Something he saw himself working at for all his days. Nothing finer than a beautiful piece of precision, keeping perfect time. And there was his training after the workday, his dreams of the Olympics. And through the feeling of it, his daughter's hand was on his, anchoring him in this world, and he was smiling, knowing she'd be there when he woke again.

Acknowledgments

I remember coming home from one of my long walks to a note from publisher Jack David offering me a contract on my first novel. It took a moment for my brain to connect to the words, and then the excitement and anticipation of the journey that I was about to embark on with ECW Press set in. And I've felt that same enthusiasm working with them on every book since.

Thank you to Jack for his steadfast support. I am truly grateful.

Everyone at ECW consistently brings their best. I'm always in good hands as each novel goes from manuscript to the bookshelves and beyond.

Thank you to Emily Schultz for her remarkable expertise. It is a privilege to work with her as my editor.

To Peter Norman, a first-rate copy editor and a stickler for detail if ever there was, thanks again.

Hats off to the folks at Made By Emblem. I love the cover for this one — they absolutely nailed it.

I also want to thank Jack David and Neil Besner for taking the time to weigh in on the Jewish and Portuguese cultural references and language.

And another nod to Jack — a while ago he sent me a news article that he thought would appeal to my sense of humor. It did. As a matter of fact, it sparked the idea for one of my favorite main characters.

And last, but certainly not least, I am forever thankful for my family, Andrea and Xander.